Gentry

(Wolves of Winter's Edge, Book 1)

T. S. JOYCE

Gentry

ISBN-13: 978-1540377197
ISBN-10: 1540377199

First electronic publication: November 2016

T. S. Joyce
www. tsjoyce.com

NOTE FROM THE AUTHOR:

This book is a work of fiction. The names, characters, places, and incidents are products of the writer's imagination or have been used fictitiously and are not to be construed as real. Any resemblance to persons, living or dead, actual events, locale or organizations is entirely coincidental. The author does not have any control over and does not assume any responsibility for third-party websites or their content.

Published in the United States of America

First digital publication: November 2016
First print publication: November 2016

Editing: Corinne DeMaagd
Cover Photography: Furious Fotog
Cover Model: Zac Smith

DEDICATION

For the Trailer Park Book Club
and beautiful, badass, sappy dragon, Roxanne.
It sure is fun watching you fly.

ACKNOWLEDGMENTS

I couldn't write these books without some amazing people behind me. A huge thanks to Corinne DeMaagd, for helping me to polish my books, and for being an amazing and supportive friend. Looking back on our journey here, it makes me smile so big. You are an incredible teammate, C! Thanks to Golden Czermak of Furious Fotog for this shot of Zac for the cover, and for being my hilarious backpack-buddy.

TnT. Y'all probably already know who I'm about to thank just from those three letters, but the other half of my signing team is Tyler Halligan, and whooo we have had some adventures. And more than that, outside of the chaos and fun of the events, he is one hell of an inspiring person.

To my family and my cubs, who put up with so much to share me with these characters, my heart is yours. You keep thanking me for working so hard for you, but that always blows my mind. You are worth every ounce of effort, no thanks needed.
You are the amazing ones.

And last but never least, thank you, awesome reader. You have done more for me and my stories than I can even explain on this teeny page. You found my books, and ran with them, and every share, review, and comment makes release days so incredibly special to me.

1010 is magic and so are you.

ONE

Gentry Striker knelt down in the snow and narrowed his eyes at the chaos he found there. Overlapping paw prints made a mess of the white ground. Crimson was splattered here and there as if painted by an artist's brush. Gentry huffed a frozen breath and lifted a handful of red snow to his nose, then sniffed it. So fresh.

The alpha of this pack was a pitch-black murder machine Gentry had deemed Tooth. Why? Because the wild wolf was missing one bottom canine. That didn't seem to hinder his ability to hurt, though. Hurt other packs, hurt his own pack, hurt animals even after he'd had his fill.

Tooth reminded Gentry of his brothers, Roman

and Asher. All three of them were grade-A, pain-in-the-ass, dominant-as-hell assholes.

Gentry had stalled on taking out Tooth, but shouldn't have. Tooth had taken yet another unnecessary victim. The pack had just fed twelve hours ago, and now they'd killed another animal, at least one… No. Gentry scented the air again. Too much blood. Maybe the pack had killed two cattle this time. The ranchers in the area wouldn't be put off anymore. Not after a month-long killing spree, and not when Tooth had grown such a fondness for the kill.

Fuck, he mouthed as he looked to the horizon, where the tree line met the deep navy sky adorned with stars. It was so beautiful here… A howl rose in the air—and so ugly all at once.

He'd memorized their voices. This one was the alpha female. He called her Eyelet because she was white with what looked like gray lace marbled into her coat. Her voice faded to nothing, then started up again. When the others in the pack didn't join, Gentry huffed a dark laugh and stood. Tonight it was then. The alpha was onto him and didn't like being hunted. Oh, the wolves knew what he was, even if the humans did not. Werewolf. They could probably smell him from a mile away. Tooth thought putting his precious Eyelet out as a lure would work on a creature like Gentry. He tossed the bloody snow to the side and strode over the crunching ground up a shallow incline. Wolf tracks were everywhere, and in the distance, the stressed bawling of cattle still sounded. They were probably against a fence on the edge of the property, eyes rolling and so wide the whites showed at the edges. A wave of protective instincts washed through him as he made his way over unmarred ground. A soft snarl rattled up his throat. Cattle shouldn't have his instincts up like this. They were prey, and he was a predator. This town had made him soft. He'd been here too long, gotten to know the people, begun to feel.

Fuck that. He was here on a job to decide which wolves needed to be culled. He would paint the snow with Tooth's blood, bring the pack under control. Wait for them to decide on a new alpha and then scare the ever-living-shit out of the wolves so they would stay far away from their new taste for beef.

Screw those whiney cattle. He wasn't here for them. He was here to get paid and to keep as many of this pack alive as he was able. Another howl rose up louder than before. He hoped he could save Eyelet. Tooth was the problem wolf here, but Eyelet would go to war for her man.

The snow sparkled a soft blue color in the moonlight, and his boots sunk in up to his ankles. Above the crunching sound of his footsteps, his phone dinged softly. Seriously? Snarling under his breath, Gentry ripped his phone out of his back pocket and checked the caller ID. Some unknown number was calling him at three in the morning.

Gentry turned it to vibrate and shoved the phone back where it belonged. Unreasonably pissed to have a hunt interrupted, he unzipped his jacket, yanked it off, and then tossed it to the ground. Balls, it was cold.

His phone was vibrating again. "I swear to God…" he muttered, prepared to curse out whatever telemarketer thought this was a good time to call.

This time the caller ID read *Roman*. What the hell? Why would his brother be calling him? They didn't talk. They weren't okay. Something rustled in the woods, and he jerked his attention to the right, but saw nothing. Roman was going to get him killed. Asshole would probably dance on his grave.

Gentry ignored the call like a champ, but right as he was pulling his shirt off to Change, a text came through.

Answer the phone, Gentry. It's dad's lawyer.

Those last three words did something awful inside of him.

Not a good time. Send.

Chest heaving, frozen breath chugging in front of his face like steam from a train, Gentry stared at the unknown number flashing across the screen again.

ANSWER THE FUCKING PHONE, Roman texted.

Gentry's fingers were already tingling with the Change, and Eyelet was still calling to him. She thought he was a real wolf and not a monster. Monsters didn't get tricked as easily, but the ghosts from his past were keeping him distracted and vulnerable. Bad place to be out here.

His phone vibrated again.

With a growl, Gentry connected the call. "What?" he murmured low.

"Gentry?" Terry Grant, Dad's long-term lawyer asked. Gentry hadn't heard his voice in years. Not since he was a kid. "I have your brothers on the phone with us."

Gentry shook his head over and over in disbelief as he scanned the woods. "Asher, too?" he asked, trying desperately to keep the hate from his voice.

"Yeah," Asher growled. "Dad's dead. Time for the prodigal son to return home."

"More tact," Terry ground out.

"Sorry," Asher said in a completely unapologetic tone. "Dad got his throat ripped out. Bled out in an alpha fight. Alone, fuck you very much. Where were you, *Favorite*?"

Dad was dead. Gentry couldn't breathe. It felt like a Mack truck was sitting on his chest, slowly crushing him, slowly suffocating him. He held his breath so they wouldn't hear it shaking and squatted down in the snow. Eyelet was still singing. She thought she was a siren. His heart was pounding too loud in his ears.

"You boys need to come home."

"That ain't home," Roman growled.

In a careful voice, Terry murmured, "It was once. You have a duty to your father. There are things that need to be settled."

"Like the pack?" Gentry asked. "Hell no."

"It's not the Striker Pack anymore, Gentry," Terry

said. "There's a new alpha."

"Who?" Asher asked.

"Rhett."

"Fuck!" Roman said too loud into the phone.

Gentry winced away. His ears were too sensitive this close to a Change.

Rhett was going to drive that pack into the ground. Probably expose them to the humans in a year or less. He was about as careful as a wild wolf. Worse even than Tooth. And Rhett had killed Dad.

A vision of Dad's charcoal gray wolf bleeding out on the sticky floor of that old Winter's Edge tavern back home made Gentry buckle in on himself. That's where the alpha fight would've been. Maybe Asher was right. Maybe he should've been there. He'd bet everything he owned Dad was only still fighting alpha wars to protect his people from Rhett. Why hadn't he told Gentry? Why had he kept quiet about it? Gentry hadn't even gotten to say goodbye.

"Stop with the snarling, Favorite," Asher gritted out. "You'll force us all to Change, and I'm in a public place. This is on you. You go home, you fix it. Roman and I are good with where we are."

"Which is where?" Gentry asked.

"Kicked out!" Roman yelled. "That's where. The destination doesn't matter, does it? When you get kicked out of your own fucking pack by your own fucking father, it doesn't matter where you are. It's all Hell. I'll be at the funeral, Terry. Whatever he left us, I don't want it. Gentry can have it all. I'll be on the first flight out of there." The line clicked.

"Same," Asher said blandly before the line clicked again.

And then there were two.

Terry sighed into the phone. "It sounds windy where you are. Your dad told me you hunt the wild wolves now. Are you hunting tonight?"

Gentry felt numb. It felt like he'd buried himself in the snow and fallen asleep, only to wake to a frostbitten body. Dad. Eyelet's howl lifted again, and this time it was close. Too close.

"I *was* hunting." Gentry swallowed hard. "Now I'm being hunted."

Gentry hung up the phone and barely resisted chucking it into the woods at the lanky black wolf with the missing tooth that stepped from the shadows.

Gentry was being hunted by wild wolves, yeah,

but that's not what he'd meant.

He was being hunted by his destiny, too.

His head wasn't in the right place for a fight right now. He was too sluggish, too slow. His inner wolf was in shock, and his insides were a tornado. Tooth, sensing weakness, bolted for him before he could even stand up. Gentry braced for impact and rolled with him, kicking up as he did and shoving Tooth behind him. *Hurry Wolf!*

His back broke. Ribs rippled and cracked like gunfire. Fingers, neck, legs, muscle, sinew, cells, everything reshaped with excruciating pain in a matter of seconds as the wolf ripped out of his skin. Tooth was already back on him, teeth clamped on his neck. That missing tooth was saving his jugular right now. No help for it, Gentry ripped away from his jaws, the pain blinding for a moment before he spun toward the alpha and engaged.

This wasn't a bar brawl, though. This wasn't one on one. It wasn't dominant monster versus the same. Wild wolves didn't understand honor. Hell, most werewolves didn't either. Out here, it was Gentry, Tooth, and the entire pack of eight that landed on him like flood waters.

Eyelet yipped a death chant.

Tooth's snarling promise of demise filled Gentry's entire mind.

And the pain had him fighting for his life.

His wolf looked just like Dad's. *Dad*. Laying there on the floor alone. Alone like Gentry.

Maybe his destiny wasn't in Rangeley like everyone had always said.

Maybe his destiny was right here.

TWO

Blaire Hayward was utterly lost, which was shocking because she could spit from one side of this teeny town to the other.

She'd passed the darned Welcome to Rangeley sign half a dozen times now and had to turn back time and time again. She still could not find the right road, and GPS was being a snarky ho who kept changing her mind on direction. It didn't help that Rangeley, Maine was one of the most confusing places on planet Earth. It was a small town, but as far as she could understand, it was made up of three villages. And possibly a plantation or two. All the signs were getting truly confounding now. The area was called the Rangeley Lakes Region because of all the bodies of water, but the more ponds and lakes she passed, the more everything started to look the same.

When the tires of her rental car slipped on the frozen road, Blaire gripped the steering wheel tighter and muttered, "Take a break, Ashlyn said. It'll be fun, Ashlyn said. I've arranged everything, Ashlyn said."

Bullcaca. Blaire was not convinced this supposed rental cabin on the outskirts of town even existed. Ashlyn had been scammed.

An older gentleman in a thick winter coat with his hands shoved deep in his pockets nodded his chin to her and stepped off the curb toward the car. Blaire slowed and rolled down the passenger's side window.

"You lost?"

Blaire's cheeks heated, and she gave a self-deprecating laugh. "Is it that obvious?"

The man's nose flared slightly as he inhaled, but his almost smile faded to a frown in an instant. "You should stay that way."

"What?"

He twitched his head in the opposite direction she was parked. "It's best if you get on to where you're going. It isn't here."

"Uuuh..." Rude. She pulled the paperwork out from under her purse on the passenger seat. "I'm looking for the Hunter Cove Inn."

The man huffed a breath and arched his bushy gray eyebrows. "No you aren't. Trust me, that place is closed to people like you."

"People like me," she murmured, glaring. What did that mean? Women? Red-heads? Non-jerk-faces? "I think I'll take my chances," she said as she rolled up her window. She could forget her manners, too.

"It's your funeral," the guy sang as he backed off from the car for her to pull away.

Now, as a rule, Blaire didn't cuss and didn't flip people off because her momma had been strict about raising her a demure lady, but that man had both her middle fingers itching to rise up.

She fought the urge, though, waved instead, gave a polite smile, and muttered, "Bye-bye now, Captain Crazy."

Saying "Hunter Cove Inn" out loud had wrestled something loose. She'd seen a sign for a Hunter Cove Wildlife Sanctuary on the other side of town. GPS was squawking like Mr. Manners for her to turn back, so she pointed her finger and poked GPS in her glowing little face to turn her off. Why? Because Blaire had traveled halfway across the country to spend a week in a secluded cabin where there was beautiful snow and scenery. That, and she hadn't taken a vacation in five years. Five. Years. She'd been going stir crazy with the stress of her job and all the drama and trauma that went down with her ex, Matt. If she was perfectly honest, she needed this. She needed a break from her life. The second her best friend and co-worker, Ashlyn, had handed her the vacation information for her birthday, something had felt right about this. Blaire never did anything crazy. She'd been an all-A student, graduated college with honors, never got rebellious in her youth other than the occasional F-bomb when she was Hulk-smash-mad. She didn't drink and had never even tried a cigarette. She'd never called into work sick, and she'd married right out of college like all her friends and family encouraged her to. She put all her efforts into being a perfect wife and perfect employee. There had been no traveling by herself or figuring out who she was outside of being a good girl. And now that Matt was gone, re-engaged way too soon if anyone asked her, she was left reeling, and finally, finally wondering who she really was outside of work and home life. A week to herself on this adventure felt right.

Plus, Ashlyn had put a lot of work into planning this trip for her. She was an amazing friend who had seen her struggling and came up with a plan. That was what she did. Ashlyn planned and got crap done, and if she saw how hard it had been on Blaire lately doing the same old thing day in and day out, then there must be a problem. Ashlyn was sensitive to everything.

"Eeeek," she squealed as she slid into the wrong lane on a sharp turn in the road. The street had been newly sanded and salted, but it was getting late in the day, the temperature was dropping, and the light snowfall was making the streets slick again.

The town was cute. Main Street wasn't huge, but it had a vast array of restaurants and specialty shops. Most houses looked like brightly-colored dollhouses, and the others were log cabins. The town was quaint. Homey even. She bet the trees around here were beautiful in the fall.

She drove along the edge of Hunter Cove Wildlife Sanctuary until she saw salvation in a sign. It was dilapidated and hanging on its side, but if she angled her head, she could read it easily enough.

Hunter Cove Inn

1010 Heath Way

A Part of Rangeley Lakes

Established in 1905

The sign sure looked old enough to be from that year. The wood was practically petrified, and the carved letters were shallow and almost unreadable, like the weather had scraped off the top several layers of the sign over time. Hopefully the cabin had been updated.

Somebody should really fix that sign, though, put it on a better post or something so tourists could read it easier. Blaire eased onto the gas and coasted down a steep, icy drive. The road wasn't long, but it wound this way and that until it dumped her into a big open parking area surrounded by three cabins, each in different stages of disrepair.

On the porch of the biggest stood a giant of a man. At least, a giant compared to her five-foot-three frame. Or perhaps he just looked tall standing up on the elevated porch. He wore thick-soled snow boots that were nice and worn-in and dark jeans. Clinging to his V-shaped torso was a heather Gray sweater so tight she could make out the ridges of his defined chest. His shoulders, too, and my oh my, his triceps were bulging from where he leaned against the front porch. A steaming mug was balanced on the railing between his hands. Up, up his bodacious bod, his neck was exposed to the cold air like winter in Maine was nothing. A tough guy then.

His face froze her in place, though. It. Was. Perfect. Sculpted jaw dusted with a five o'clock shadow, dirty blond hair, short on the sides and gelled on top. Strong, straight nose, and sensual lips even when they were frowning, like right now. His eyes were the true shock. They were the most stunning shade of green.

Oh shit, she was still moving! Blaire whipped the car into a parking spot in front of him as though she'd meant to be like some speedy bad-A, and then smiled timidly at him through the front window. She even waved, but his frown only deepened. Pity, he probably looked even cuter when he smiled. Mission possible, she accepted her own personal smile challenge.

"Hidey ho!" she called, stepping from the car. Hidey ho? God. Blaire shook her head and wished for the millionth time in her life she didn't blush so easily. Stupid fair skin. She cleared her throat and tried again. "I'm here for the cabin rental."

The sexpot jerked so hard he knocked the mug off the railing. Quick as a whip, he reached out and snatched it out of thin air. By the handle. Hot coffee splashed onto the snow near the porch.

"Whoa," she murmured. "That was some kind of ninja move." Ninjas were sexy.

The man stood ramrod straight and hid the mug behind his back. "Uh, I think you have the wrong place." His voice was a deep baritone that vibrated from her ears to her chest to her nethers.

"Why does everyone keep saying I'm in the wrong place?" She leaned into the rental to pull out the paperwork, then shoved it up at him. "Look, my friend rented this place for a week."

The man's eyes narrowed to striking green slits. "I'm not looking for a week-long renter. The ad was supposed to be for something more permanent. Maybe for someone willing to put some work into this place, or, I don't know..." He ran his hand up the back of his head and stared off at the frozen lake behind the other two cabins. "Just take care of it so I don't have to."

"Oh." Blaire looked around the property with new eyes. There were stacks of paint buckets on a sheet of plastic on the porch and a bunch of tools spread out over a porch swing. "Well, I traveled a long way to get here, and it's paid for. Can I stay this week, and you worry about getting a long-term renter when I leave?"

"Uuuh, I don't think that's a good idea."

"Why?"

"Because you're..."

"I'm what?" she asked loudly, utterly frustrated by the men in this weird town.

The man puffed air out his cheeks and leaned his hip against the porch railing. Fine, he could give her the silent treatment all he wanted. With a growl, she yanked the giant purple suitcase from the backseat and bullied it toward the stairs.

"What are you doing?"

"I'm"—she yanked the suitcase up two stairs—"moving"—two more stairs, and she almost fell but saved herself—"in!" She stumbled onto the porch and settled her suitcase on its wheels.

She had come in hot and nearly ran into Giant Sexypotamus her hand out for a shake. She blew a red-gold curl out of her face and said, "I'm Blaire Hayward, nice to meet you." Whoa, he smelled good. She sniffed. It was some kind of cologne. He still wouldn't take her hand and was looking at her as if she'd lost her mind. Ridiculous man.

Blaire snatched his limp hand and pumped it a few times. "And your name is?"

"Gentry. Gentry."

"Cool names, but my momma said never trust a man with two first names."

A tiny smirk took his lips as he looked down at their still clasped hands. "No, it's Gentry Striker."

"Your last name is Striker? Your middle name is Badass, isn't it? Or wait! Gentry Chaos Striker. Am I close?"

Gentry removed his hand from hers and almost, almost smiled when he said, "You're an odd one, Blaire Hayward."

There were much worse things he could've said, so she offered him a prim, "Thank you," and dragged her suitcase across the uneven flooring toward the door.

"Unless you feel like sleeping in my room, you may want to divert that big-ass suitcase of yours toward the cabin over there." He pointed to the smallest one with the newest looking paint that sat across the parking lot, closest to the frozen lake.

"Right. Is there a key?"

"Nobody locks doors around here."

"Okay then. The paperwork said three meals a day. Shall we eat them in the big cabin?" she asked innocently. She'd just made that part up.

"Uh, if you like macaroni for every meal, you're welcome to beg food." That sexy little smirk was back like he knew she was bullcrapping him.

Blaire gave him a coy smile, which probably made her look like a gremlin because she hadn't flirted in a very long time, and then bounced and bumped the suitcase down the stairs behind her. She made it approximately five feet across the snowy parking lot before the luggage was pulled from her hand and one sexy Gentry Striker went striding by her, holding the heavy case like it weighed nothing. Hoowee, and he was strong? His sweater sat right at his hips so she could see his firm butt moving with each step.

"Are you checking out my ass, Ms. Hayward?" he called, as if he had eyes in the back of his head. She checked to make sure, but nope, he just had sexy, mussed hair.

"I would never," she said, then pursed her lips to hide her smile as she followed promptly behind him.

Why was her stomach doing flip-flops? Probably because she hadn't eaten dinner. "Hey, where is a good place to eat around here?"

Gentry cast her a quick, unreadable glance over his shoulder. It was just a flash of those green eyes, and then he gave her his back again. "This town closes down pretty early during winter."

"Okay, but there has to be somewhere I can get some dinner. You don't want to see me when I'm hangry," she said in a Hulk voice.

She giggled. He did not.

Gentry led her up a few stairs, across a small porch with a single rocking chair, and into the cabin. "Look, if you're going to stay here, you need to stay inside after dark."

"No thanks, I'm here to vacation not be locked up

as soon as the sun goes down. And I'm really hungry. I haven't eaten since breakfast."

Gentry made a deep rattling noise in his throat, but cut it off quick and looked real busy settling her suitcase by the front door. "Tell me what kind of food you like, and I'll go get it for you." Through gritted teeth, he said, "It's the least I can do since I'm fresh out of macaroni."

Blaire's stubbornness warred with her desire to actually see if this big hunky man would feed her. "I want a chili dog. No! I want a bacon burger with fries and a side of ranch and extra pickles on the burger. And a shake. Something pink. Strawberry or cherry."

"Great. I'll be back."

"Money!" She scrambled into her purse as he waited by the door looking wholly uncomfortable. She gave him a twenty. "Grab something for yourself too, Chaos."

"That's not my name, and I already ate." He yanked the twenty from her fingertips and made his way out the door.

His sexy scent still lingered so she closed her eyes and inhaled noisily. And when she sighed happily and opened them again, she was mortified to find Gentry standing in the doorway.

The ghost of that smirk was back. "One side of ranch or two."

Cheeks on fire, she tried to regain her composure as she squeaked out, "Always two."

"You got it Blaire Trouble Hayward." And then Gentry stepped back into the darkening evening.

This time, out the front window, Blaire watched him leave. Gentry jogged around to the back of the big cabin. A minute later, he pulled an old brown and white refurbished Ford truck with chains on the tires around the side and zoomed up the road and out of sight.

Her, trouble? Heck nope, she was still a good girl.

But there was a hundred percent chance that man was trouble with a capital T.

THREE

What the hell was he doing? Gentry stopped at the light and shook his head for the tenth time since he'd left Hunter Cove. Blaire being in this town right now was a bad idea for about a dozen reasons.

One: she was human. Fragile. Paper-thin skin, and the single bite of a werewolf could kill her. Hell, a splinter could kill her. Humans died too easily, and this town was a steel trap with a hundred razor-sharp teeth.

Two: she was a fucking human! He shouldn't even be physically attracted to humans, but here he was, adjusting his hard dick because God, she was a stunner. It made no sense. Werewolves liked other werewolves. That's just the way it was. They were genetically predisposed to seek out a mate who could bear them werewolf pups. Blaire was a genetic dead-end for his kind. She would have fragile, little human babies only. *Down dick.*

Three: he was right in the middle of funeral arrangements for Dad, pissed as hell, had been forced to put down Tooth and half his damn pack to survive, was on the verge of a Change constantly, and his dickhole brothers were slowing everything down by staying MIA. Taking care of a human on top of the pile other shit he had going on was a horrible idea. He would slip up. He would get her killed. Or fuck, he could be the one doing the killing if he didn't rein in his wolf as soon as fuckin' possible.

Gentry gassed it at the green light and skidded onto Main Street. The tavern would have the food she wanted.

Four: Rhett.

Five: the newly named Bone-Ripper Pack was going through a huge transition, out from under Dad, who had been a good alpha, to under Rhett's control. There would be violence.

Six: Rangeley was the home of one of the biggest packs in the world. And the people who weren't werewolves here were all unsuspecting humans. It needed to stay that way. Already the wolves walked such a fine line in this town, and now Blaire had stepped right into the middle of the chaos.

Seven: the raging boner. Yep, that one got an extra number because it was really confusing, and Blaire felt like trouble. Big trouble. His wolf was showing signs of wanting to settle, and he couldn't have that. And here came this drop-dead gorgeous human woman, red-gold hair cascading down her shoulders in wild curls like she'd come off some Scottish moor. Green eyes, but slanted like a cat. Fair skin, almost the color of the snow, and a light dusting of freckles on her cheeks. Curves for fuckin' days. Big, soft titties pushing against a little, white sweater that said she was completely confident with her figure. Nice ass hugged by tight skinny jeans. That ass was more than a handful, and his hands were big. He'd wanted to reach out and squeeze it so hard when she'd pranced past him with her suitcase. And she smelled like jasmine and honeysuckle. She smelled like spring in the dead of dark winter.

"Cut it out, Striker," he growled.

In a parking space facing the Four Horsemen's

Tavern, he let the truck idle and rested his elbow on the edge of the window as he bit the corner of his thumbnail, a habit he'd picked up as a kid and had never curbed. There was no way he was going in there hard. He didn't even know any other wolves who had been attracted to a human. Blaire was a danger, and in danger in this town, and he'd just invited her to stay for a week? He was going to fillet the rental management company that fucked this up. The last thing he needed was to babysit a temporary renter when all he wanted to do was escape this place. It was a big mistake to give him a week-long renter instead of the year contract he'd requested, and he couldn't handle anything extra right now. He needed to tie up loose ends, spread Dad's ashes to the wind, and leave Rangeley forever, just like he'd planned.

Rangeley was quicksand to a roamer like him. He couldn't get stuck. Wouldn't get stuck. Already he could feel the cold, dead claws of his destiny clamping onto his ankle, and he needed to buck them off as fast as he could.

Blaire, Blaire, with the wild red hair. She was funny, too. Didn't have a filter. Said what came to her mind. He liked that. No games. And when he'd caught her sniffing the air like she was a wolf, like she was a creature of the night like him, he'd found her so damn amusing. And so beautiful—eyes closed, shimmery make-up glistening in the soft light, dark eyelashes resting on cheeks that had turned rosy from the cold or a blush. He hoped it was a blush. If she blushed easily, he could tell when he shocked her. He could play games and see how far he could push her before she pushed back. Wolf games, but with a human. Cat and mouse. Dog and cat. Big bad wolf and little red. He forced himself to stop smiling. That was a fucked-up thought. He wouldn't be the one trying to gobble her up. He needed to get her out of Rangeley and out of his head as soon as possible. She could stay the night, but tomorrow he had to figure out a way to make her leave.

Boner tamed, Gentry shoved his door open and grabbed his jacket on the passenger's seat. This was the act. He shrugged into the thick winter coat like he needed it, and like he didn't run hot as a furnace, so the humans in this town didn't pay him any extra attention.

After he slammed the door closed, Gentry jogged

across the parking lot, his hands shoved into his pockets. The second he yanked open the door, though, he regretted choosing the Four Horsemen for Blaire's dinner. The stink of werewolf hit him like a wrecking ball.

A soft snarl clawed its way up the back of his throat as he scanned the room. Clearly, Rhett had chased the humans from the bar since it was all supes. Fuck. Everyone was gathered around the bar, having a pack meeting probably, but had all stopped talking and were now twisted around, staring back at him. Most of them he recognized. Some of them he was happy to see again, some of them not. It was an odd sensation seeing his old pack, yet everything was different. Everyone was older, harder. There were no smiles like there used to be. Only snarled-up lips and threatening growls.

He was *other* now.

"Gentry Striker," Rhett called out from behind the bar where he was leaning on locked arms. "You come here for the same fate I gave your dad?"

Gentry wanted to kill him. He wanted to do it slowly. He wanted to watch him gasp for air and whimper in pain and bleed out on the floor in front of everyone. He wanted Rhett to die looking at his face. He wanted to avenge Dad, but that wasn't how shit worked for werewolves. He was supposed to get over it instead, move on, find his place in a pack or as a rogue, let Rhett keep his alpha victory.

But all Gentry could think of was Dad lying on the floor with Rhett's ugly wolf shredding him, and he wanted revenge so bad his mouth watered and tasted like blood.

But it was him versus the Bone-Ripper Pack, and he was a more careful hunter than that, so he exposed his neck like a good little werewolf and made his way slowly toward the to-go stand near the kitchen.

Mila was there, pretty as ever. Timid as ever. He was kind of surprised she was still living in this town after Dad died. He'd protected her. Now she would be a piñata for a bully like Rhett. He didn't do well with submissives. He never had.

"It's good to see you again," Mila whispered, her chin dropped to her chest, hands shaking as she opened up a computer screen behind the counter. He'd almost cared for the dainty dark-haired beauty once, back when he'd believed in that destiny shit.

His life could've been laid out like a straight-line road map. Stay here, choose Mila as a mate, have a half dozen pups, take the pack when Dad was ready to give it up, petrify like an old gnarled tree.

Mila had never called to his wolf enough to keep in him this place, though.

No one had.

He forced a smile, the pack in his peripheral, always at the edge of his vision because survivors didn't turn their back on danger like that. "It's good to see you, too." He almost meant it. He'd never planned on seeing any of these people again.

Gentry put in his order and sat on the last barstool. None of the wolves were talking, just watching. Every hair on his body had electrified, but tucking tail and running would only send them after him faster. Posturing was everything in a pack.

Slowly, Gentry took off his jacket, reached over the bar, pulled out a bottle of Jim Beam and a shot glass, poured one, and slammed it. He looked Rhett directly in his stupid fucking eyes and growled, "What?"

"You lost? Pack meeting, and you weren't invited because you're not pack. In fact," Rhett barked out, "you're the bloodline of the defeated last alpha, so I have a right to snuff you out of existence right here and now."

Gentry arched his eyebrow. "I'd dare you to challenge me, but I don't want the pack. I'm here to take care of my dad's shit, and I'll be gone as soon as I possibly can. Wasn't really my choice coming back, Rhett."

"You could've let me know you were in town. That's the respectful thing to do—"

"That would imply," Gentry said loudly, "that I have respect for you. You aren't my alpha. I don't have to do shit for you." Gentry held his gaze as he replaced the bottle of Jim Beam behind the counter.

"Frank's rushing your order," Mila said breathlessly from the other side of the bar.

"Mila!" Rhett barked out, like she'd done something wrong.

A long, high-pitched whine sounded from her. A no-no if she'd done it in public around humans. She was standing behind the to-go stand, wringing her hands, looking down at the floor.

"Get over here," Rhett said in a voice too gravelly and dangerous for Gentry's liking.

Gentry didn't have feelings for the woman, but he sure as shit didn't like seeing her treated like dirt. He'd watched Rhett treat women like crap from the time the asshole had shown up to right before Gentry had left town.

Mila approached the muscled-up alpha slowly.

"Now!"

She jumped and pushed her legs faster, then came to stand under his outstretched arm.

Rhett smiled a predatory look at Gentry.

"Don't," Gentry warned him.

Eyes locked on him, Rhett leaned down and kissed Mila, trapping her with the crook of his arm. Mila struggled for a second, then remembered herself and stood stock still, lips pursed and stiff.

Gentry lost his mind. Just...lost it. He threw the shot glass before he even realized he'd done it. Right before it slammed into Rhett's face, a hand blurred out and plucked it from the air, turned it right side up in one smooth motion and slammed it onto the countertop.

Rhett shoved Mila away from him, fury roiling in his eyes, and opened his mouth. Before he could get a word out, Dad's best friend, Tim, the one who'd saved the alpha's face from the glass, was on Gentry. For a split second, in the moment Tim's fist connected with Gentry's jaw, he felt a potent sting of betrayal. Tim had watched him grow up, and now he was protecting that asshole. But his punch was too soft. *Make this believable*, Tim's eyes pleaded as they went to the floor.

Fuck, he was going to have to do this. He was going to have to fight Tim because he was right. If Gentry wasn't put in his place by Tim, Rhett would have the entire pack wailing on him. So he did make it believable. Gentry went to blows with the old man until they were breathless and bleeding. Until Gentry couldn't see out of his right eye, and crimson streamed down Tim's face. Until two of the tables in the bar were broken and four chairs toppled. Until Tim kicked him in the ribs, and he heard the distinct snap of one breaking.

Gentry wasn't down and out, but he could look weak. Rhett didn't have to know he'd kept his body in fighting shape. He didn't have to know he was a wild wolf hunter. Gentry curled in on himself, arm slung around his ribcage. He groaned a pained sound and spat red onto the floor. "Fuck."

Tim backed off, but in the fluorescent lighting, he looked green, like he would retch. Well, welcome to the club. Gentry hated that fight, too.

"Get out," Tim snarled.

Rhett was laughing, and so were some of the others.

"Damn, Striker," Rhett crowed. "You never really had a shot at alpha, did you? You just got your ass kicked by an old man." And then his voice lost its amusement as he growled out, "You look like your dad lying there."

Those words caused something dark to churn inside of Gentry. That shouldn't make sense. Alpha challenges were done as wolves. But this ugly, awful vision of Rhett fighting his dad human flashed across his mind, and once it was there, it wouldn't let go. Something was off. Something was wrong.

Standing over him, Tim flashed a warning with his gray-sky eyes.

Gentry swallowed hard and struggled up, then limped out the door, daring to give the pack his back. Daring to give Rhett his exposed neck and spine.

"Leave town quickly before you become ashes in the wind like your old man," Rhett called out.

His mind spun like a top as he made his way outside and let the door swing closed behind him. It was snowing harder now, big, white, fluffy flakes. His body was running too hot with the urge to Change and rip that motherfucker's throat out. He sighed and held out his hands, lifted his face to the black sky and closed his eyes against the cold. It seeped into his bones and cooled the fury in his blood with each steadying breath he took. Is this what he was now? Fighting old friends to survive the man who'd killed his father? All he had in the world was pride, and Rhett had just ripped it from him in front of the people he used to care about.

"Psst."

Gentry inhaled deeply and opened his eyes. Mila stood at the corner of the building with a bag of food. She set it down in the snow in front of her boots. Tears were streaming down her cheeks and dripping from her jaw line.

"That was supposed to be you," she said, her voice shaking. "You could've saved us." He'd never seen her angry enough to hold anyone's gaze, much less a dominant's like his. Before she turned around the corner, she uttered, "I loved your father, but I hate you, Gentry Striker." She held his gaze a second longer before she disappeared.

He understood hate. He felt it all the time. For his brothers. For Rhett. For this town.

It hurt being the one who was hated, though.

He texted Asher and Roman. *Where the fuck are you?*

He made his way to the food, yanked it out of the snow, and strode for his truck. Someone had bashed in his headlights and broken his windshield into a spiderweb of glass. Fuckin' pack.

He ground his teeth against the growl that snarled up from his aching chest. His whole body hurt from not defending himself like he wanted in that fight. Gentry tossed the bag of food onto the passenger's seat, shut the door beside him, and glared at the Four Horsemen. And then he screamed for as long and as loud as his broken rib would allow.

He pulled out of the parking lot. Asher and Roman wouldn't answer his text. They never had before. He was the responsible one, the one who got shit done, the one who took care of the hard stuff. It had always been like that, but it shouldn't be this way now. They weren't punk kids anymore. They were grown. All he needed was for them to show up so they could spread Dad's ashes and go on with the rest of their lives.

Blaire would leave tomorrow. He would make it happen, but right now, he wished to God he could make that happen for himself, too.

FOUR

Okay…now what?

Blaire looked around the cabin living room expectantly. She'd put away all her things in the single bedroom, hung her sweaters by color, organized the drawers, placed her shoes just so in the closet, put all her toiletries in neat lines on the counter in the bathroom, and was dressed in her sexiest pajamas. By sexiest, she meant a long-sleeved purple sleep shirt with cartoon llamas printed on them and matching thermal leggings. There was a zero percent chance of her getting laid if Gentry saw her in these, so when a sudden knock echoed through the door, she startled hard, almost spilling her glass of red wine, and then only opened the barrier between them a crack.

Only Gentry didn't stay outside, but shoved his way in and paced along the back wall like a wild animal in a cage.

Blaire tiptoed toward the throw blanket folded neatly on the back of the moose-print couch.

"Stop right there. Don't come any closer."

Blaire froze, mid sip of her wine. When he turned and paced the other way, she got a good look at his face, which was swollen and bloody, and why was he limping?

"What happened to you?" she exclaimed as she approached him.

She cornered him good, and he backed up to the wall, face averted, but she wasn't going to be put off. "You're bleeding," she murmured, touching the short whiskers on his jaw.

Gentry grabbed her wrist. "What part confused you, woman? Stop right there, or don't come any closer?"

Blaire gulped her wine because, truth be told, she'd filled it to the tippy top, and it was sloshing. "Who did this?"

Gentry took the glass from her hand and downed

the rest like a shot. Okay then.

She tried to pull his face toward her again, but he swatted her hand away like a pesky fly. "Stop touching me, Trouble. You're making everything worse."

"I'm making it worse? I didn't beat you, and I shared my wine with you. You're very welcome, sir."

Gentry dragged a quick glance down her pajamas and then back up to her face. At least he didn't laugh, but it was rather rude when he said, "I've thought about it, and you need to leave tomorrow."

"No."

Gentry looked slapped. "What?"

"I said no. The cabin is paid for, I'm not leaving my vacation, so stop being a butthole."

One blond brow arched up. "I'm sorry, did you just call me a butthole?"

"I don't cuss."

He looked down at her pajamas again. "Are those llamas?"

"Don't judge, I didn't invite you in here. I thought you were going to pass me the food through the crack I made in the door. Wait, where is the food?" The panic set in a little. She wasn't good just devouring wine on an empty stomach, and already she was feeling tipsy. "You're bleeding for mysterious reasons, and there is no food. Gentry, I was serious about being hungry, and what happened to your face? Did you have a bad drug deal or a bar fight or an accident?"

"B."

"What?" she asked, dumbfounded.

"Option B—the bar fight one."

"Oh. Fantastic."

"I got food. I just left it in the truck. This was a bad idea." Slowly, he covered his crotch with his hands.

Heat blazed up her neck and landed in her cheeks as she backed off a few steps. Well, this was awkward. He made her horny, too, but she was a girl and could hide it better. "I'm going to..."

"You aren't wearing a bra..."

She lifted her empty glass in the air. "Get some more wine."

"Your nipples are..."

"You better be about to say 'glorious' and not 'big,'" she muttered, walking away. She wasn't wearing underwear either because vacation, but he didn't have to know that.

"Are you not wearing panties either?"

"I told you I wasn't trying to invite you in!"

The wine bottle glugged and emptied completely as she filled it to the tip-top again. She even waited for the last few drops to shake into it before she took a long sip.

"You weren't supposed to say no." There was a frown in his deep, sexy voice.

"Does every woman tell you yes? That sounds boring, and quite frankly, it's probably why you're still single." Yep, she was fishing. She sipped her wine and arched her eyebrows primly as she waited for a response.

Disappointingly, he didn't take the bait. Instead, he strode directly for the door and disappeared outside. The swinging door banged closed, startling her all over again. Gentry wasn't a gentle man. He was stompy, and moved too fast, and didn't care about nearly breaking everything. Maybe he didn't know his own strength or something. Blaire craned her neck to watch him walk with his long, deliberate strides to his truck parked in front of her cabin. He would probably break her in the bedroom. Rough man. Probably spanked too hard, nibbled too roughly, grabbed too firmly, and thrusted…too…deeply.

Blaire narrowed her eyes at his back. Gentry had turned her into a pervert.

When he made his way up the steps with a bulging bag of food, she pretended to be reading one of the outdoor magazines that had been stacked in the middle of the counter. Something about knives, or stalking coyotes, or duck calls, or she didn't know. The second Gentry opened the door again, he filled the entire room. How did he do that? It was as if her body were hyper-aware of him.

She'd never had this kind of physical reaction to anyone, not even Matt, and she'd really loved him once.

Was this lust? Was this what Ashlyn had been talking about? She'd been trying to get Blaire to go out and party for months and encouraged hook-ups with men, but she hadn't been ready. Maybe she still wasn't emotionally, but now her body seemed ready enough to do dirty deeds with one sexy-as-hell Gentry Striker.

Gentry parted those sensual lips as though he wanted to say something, but instead, he leaned down, set the bag of food in the middle of the floor, and gruffly said, "Goodnight, Trouble."

Mmm, she liked that he had given her a nickname as if they were old friends, but she did not like that he'd put her food down like she was a rabid raccoon and then bolted from the house like he couldn't escape her fast enough.

She padded over to the bag, saw there was way more than she'd ordered, and bolted for the snow boots she'd left by the door. She shoved her feet into them and sprinted outside with the food. Dang, Gentry was fast. He was already to his cabin across the parking area, so she had to run. Her boots crunched through the snow, and she slipped twice on the layer of ice beneath it, but she got within yelling distance before he closed the door.

"Wait! Aaah!" She slipped again and splayed her legs for balance.

In his open doorway, Gentry wore the deepest frown she'd ever seen on a person. "What are you doing?"

Huffing cold breath, she made her way in front of his porch like she was Romeo and he was Juliet. Dramatically, she spread her arms out, food dangling from one hand. "You're alone, and I'm alone, and you left your food in here, and it's my birthday. And holy shrimp, it's cold out here. I'm regretting the no-jacket..."

"Still no bra..."

"I think I'm getting frostbite. The world is going dark." Blaire coughed delicately.

"Jesus," he muttered, but he did seem to be fighting a teeny, tiny smile. "Is it really your birthday, or are you bullshitting me?"

She was shivering and really uncomfortable. Slowly, she covered her nipples, which had drawn up like little marbles against the thin material of her pajamas. "This vacation was a last-minute thing. It was a birthday present from my best friend. Today is really my big day. Dirty thirty."

"Dirty thirty? You're thirty years old?"

"Why are you looking at me like that?"

"Well, first off, I thought you were mid-twenties max, and two, I thought fancy women like yourself didn't give your age readily."

"How old are you?" she asked through chattering teeth.

"Twenty-Six."

"Oh." She didn't know why, but she'd pegged him as the same age as her, or maybe a couple years older. He was so confident and gave off this air of maturity that had tricked her. He was all tall and strong and, for reasons beyond her comprehension, he made her feel safe.

But…he was younger. She had no chance in hell with a young buck like him.

Whoa, where had that thought come from? She was here for a week, nothing more. She wasn't looking for a "young buck."

Gentry didn't look happy about it, but he twitched his chin in an inviting gesture and held the door open wider.

Sexy, and he hadn't uttered a single word.

Blaire scrambled up the porch stairs and hustled inside, but not before she subtly sniffed him again as she passed. "What cologne do you use?" she asked nonchalantly. She wanted to bathe in the stuff.

"Uh, no cologne. It's a body spray." Gentry closed the door and made his way to the fireplace. "This place doesn't have central heat and air, sorry," he muttered. While he built a fire in the hearth as if he'd done it a billion times, Blaire scanned the big cabin.

She hadn't known what to expect, but it wasn't this. The cabin was very old, but had been kept up. The wood logs exposed on the ceiling were faded to a soft brownish-gray, but were polished to shining. The entryway led directly into a living area with an open kitchen on the right. In the center of the great room was the old stone hearth Gentry was currently building a fire in. The hearth was off-kilter, and none of the stones were uniform. Some stuck out farther, some sunk in. The chimney was made of the same kind of rock as it crawled up, up into the unique log rafters. A stone staircase curved up behind it and disappeared into a hallway. The railing was made of thin tree stumps and winding branches that gave this place a feeling of old and new. Old-fashioned sconces glowed invitingly on either side of a set of French doors on the back wall that showed the picturesque winter woods outside. There was no television, no electronics of any kind that she could see. Just two chairs and a couch in the middle of the great room that faced each other, and a couple of small end tables near them. The floors were scuffed and looked refurbished, like everything else in here. It was the most beautiful home she'd ever seen, which was strange, because she'd never been a fan of cabins in particular. She liked homes that looked like dollhouses.

"My dad lived here," Gentry said from right behind her.

She startled because she hadn't heard him approach. She jumped again when he dropped a blanket over her shoulders. Gentry frowned and backed off a few steps. "I wouldn't hurt you."

"Sorry," she murmured. "I got a little lost in this place for a second."

Gentry cast a quick glance around, then rolled the sleeves of his sweater up as though he was hot. Impossible since this place was almost as cold as it was outside. "My dad called it ten-ten. Said there was magic in this place."

"Do you believe in magic?" she asked.

"No. I believe in survival, that's all." Gentry took the bag of food from her hand and led her to the hearth. He scooted a chair loudly across the floor and faced it to the flames, then gestured for her to take a seat. And after he'd done the same to a second chair, sat down, and propped his feet on the ledge of the hearth, he handed her the cold food she'd ordered.

"You want to talk about what happened to your face?"

"Nope," he clipped out.

"Just making sure it wasn't something you…you know…needed to get off your chest. For some people getting hit can be something hurtful. I mean, maybe it's different for guys." Blaire shrugged self-consciously.

He cast her an unreadable glance and then bit into a hamburger of his own. "You ever been hit?"

"Me? Oh, no, I wasn't talking about me." She ate a few fries and watched the flames for a bit. "My mom got hit a few times by my dad before she threw him out. The last time, she locked us in my room. I was sixteen, and I held her while she cried. I knew at the time she was in her own head saying goodbye to him. I held her until she fell asleep against me, and I hated him for what he did because I knew the pain she felt in her face was nothing compared to the pain and distrust that would be in her heart for a long time. We chased him out after that, and I never talked to him again. But I watched my mom's recovery, and I just wanted to make sure those cuts on your face weren't hurting your heart, too."

"Your mom sounds like a tough lady."

"She is."

Gentry relaxed back into his chair and sighed. "Nothing touches my heart, Blaire. You don't have to worry about me. Blood is a part of my life. Pain, too. I was used to it before I could even walk. It was just a barfight, nothing dramatic."

"Okay," she said, shutting down like he'd shut down.

They ate in silence for a few minutes before he sighed, which tapered into a feral sound as he leaned forward. He dropped his leftover food into the bag on the floor and clasped his hands, then slid her a narrow-eyed glance. "I used to live here. The dynamics have changed. The leadership in the town has shifted, and they don't appreciate me being back. I'm a threat, so..." He gestured to his face.

"So they had to put you in your place."

"Exactly."

"That blows."

He huffed a breath in an almost-laugh. "Everything about this place blows. My wo—" Gentry swallowed down whatever word he was going to say and tried again. "I'm ready to move on already, and I just got here. I like to roam."

"Ramblin' man."

"Yep."

"I'm the opposite of you, Gentry Striker. I will dig my roots so hard and so deep into a place I will grow stagnant and not move or breathe or think for years."

"But you're here."

She gave him a tired smile. "I'm trying to break my roots."

"Why?"

"Divorce."

"Oh, shit. When?"

"A year ago."

"So you're still in the man-hating phase then," he said with a baiting smile.

Blaire giggled. She couldn't help it. This wasn't funny at all, but… "Yeah, I guess I am. You suck less than the other boys, though."

"So far."

"Yeah, you still have a whole week to make me hate you. Better get to practicing."

"What should I do?"

"Uuuuh, you could ignore me. You could slowly grow colder and more distant until you barely look at me. You could call me names. You could make me feel invisible."

Gentry's lip curled up in a terrifying grimace. Just a second, and then it was gone, as if it had never been there before. But she'd seen it, and the feral expression had lifted the hairs on the back of her neck.

"Is that what your ex did?"

Blaire inhaled deeply and nodded. "Pretty lame. I always thought the only way I would ever consider divorce was if he hit me or he cheated. Our break was quiet, though. No drama. He just gave me the papers one day, and after the shock wore off, we both just...left. We'd been together since we were kids, and married young. When we divorced, he told me he didn't know if he ever loved me, or if he just needed someone to love him like I did when we were younger. He told me he didn't need that anymore. Didn't need me. He didn't want kids, and that made it worse because I want to be a mom. We hugged goodbye the day he moved out of the house. No yelling, no name-calling. It was like two roommates going on with their lives. Only he moved on, and I grew my roots deeper. Clung to the house and all our pictures. All of our memories. I dug my claws into work so it would distract me from the ache, and at some point, I lost myself completely. So here I am in Rangeley…"

"Trying to find yourself again," Gentry finished in a deep rumble.

She nodded and stared at the flickering fire. "Yep."

"That's why you said 'no' when I asked you to leave."

"Yeah, I kind of need this week."

Gentry cracked his knuckles and shook his head. He gave her a sideways glance, and she could've sworn his green eyes were brighter somehow. "There are things you don't understand here. Things under the surface."

"Danger?"

He dipped his chin once. "If you stay, you listen if I ask you to do stuff, no questions asked."

She stiffened at that. "I don't like being told what to do."

"I bet you don't. I don't like telling people what to do. It's why I left this place when I was a kid. I was supposed to be a leader here."

"Like the mayor?"

His eyes narrowed. "Something like that. I won't try and boss you around, Blaire, but I'm not very popular in town right now. You're staying at my inn, and I don't want any of the tension to blow back on you. So please, if I ask you to do something, just do it. Okay?"

Blaire lifted her attention to the cuts and bruises on the left side of his face. There was no reason to trust him, but Gentry had made sure she'd stayed in the cabin tonight instead of going out to get food, and look what had happened to him. She believed he was protecting her in some confusing way, even though he had no reason to. And now, he was asking her to trust him.

"Okay," she agreed quietly.

She didn't understand what was happening here in Rangeley, but she had a bone-deep instinct that Gentry had his finger on the pulse of this town. He was offering to keep her out of trouble, and all the lust she felt toward him gave way just a little to something more. In this moment, with his bright green eyes locked on her, a soft expression on his usually hard face, one of her thin heartstrings that had somehow survived her ex latched tentatively to Gentry.

This was the most terrifying moment of her life. She didn't want another break, and getting attached to a man was setting her up for just that. This had been fun when she'd just been turned on by him, but this conversation had changed the winds and sent their little boat crashing sideways into a wave.

"I should go," she murmured, trying to hold a tight smile.

Gentry's eyebrows lowered into a troubled expression, but he nodded. "Probably best."

"Goodnight, Gentry," she said, standing. She set the wadded-up food wrapper in the bag and moved to take the blanket off her shoulders, but Gentry was there so fast she gasped. His hands pressed on her shoulders, keeping the blanket in place.

"Bring it back later when you decide to wear a damn jacket outside." His voice was too gruff, too rough, too low.

He pressed his body against hers, and his hands tightened slightly on her shoulders. The flames from the hearth heated her front while Gentry warmed her back. God, she should be running from him. She should be sprinting to her car and peeling out of here, out of this town, out of the reach of this tempting man.

But her body, the traitor, stood there frozen and wanting. With his cheek, Gentry pushed her head to the side gently, then lowered his mouth to her neck and brushed it there as soft as a butterfly kiss. Parting her lips, Blaire let off a helpless sound and rolled her eyes closed against how good it felt to be touched by a man again.

Gentry inhaled deeply right at her hair line. The short whiskers on his jaw raised gooseflesh up her body. He was teasing with a kiss on her neck, letting his lips touch her, then easing away. He scraped his facial scruff across her sensitive skin, then eased away again. His hands slid from her shoulders down her back to her hips. Slowly, he pulled the blanket from her and pressed his body more firmly against her back. And oh, she could feel his excitement against her spine. A soft noise whispered from his throat that sounded animalistic. She liked it.

Gentry slid his left hand around her hipbone, brushing his fingertips just under the hem of her shirt, dragging fire where his skin touched hers. She inhaled sharply and rolled back against him instinctively. The second she moved against him, he grabbed her hard, digging his fingers into her skin. Rough man, just like she knew he would be.

"Don't tempt me to take this too far tonight, Trouble," he murmured against her neck.

Ooooh he was a sexy talker, teasing her, making promises, hinting that he had plans. She wanted to tempt him, so she rolled her body back against his again.

Gentry's hand slid smoothly up her shirt and cupped her breast, and dear goodness nothing had felt better. Nothing in her entire life. He kneaded her gently, and with his other hand, he brushed his fingertips just under the elastic of her waistband.

"Tell me to stop, Trouble," he dared her, then plucked gently against her neck with his lips. He still hadn't kissed her. Only teased with his mouth.

They should stop. She was supposed to be bolting out the door and putting space between them before she fell harder. Even if she felt like she knew him, and even if she trusted him in ways that made no sense, he was still a danger to her heart. But he was touching her, feeling her, working her into an inferno. Warmth pooled in her belly, and she was already wet from what he'd done to her body. Gentry was a man who knew how to touch a woman, and maybe she needed this.

She should've told him to stop, but instead she cupped her hand over his and guided him down into her pants. Gentry wasn't teasing anymore. He slid his finger right inside of her, then let off a shuddering breath as if it felt as good to him as it did to her. He pulled out and pushed back in, hitting her clit. Geez, this was everything. Her body was overheating from the flames in the hearth or from Gentry's body warmth or from the fire he'd created inside of her. Maybe all three. Her sensitive nerve endings sparked like lightning every time he slid into her just right. She reached over her shoulder and gripped the back of his neck, holding him close as he worked her toward release. Almost there already.

"Gentry," she whispered, begging for something she didn't understand. He was already giving her everything. "Oooh," she moaned as he pushed into her again.

His lips were back on her neck, just barely, brushing her skin, so close to a kiss. She'd never been withheld a kiss before. She loved and hated it. She wanted it, wanted him to lock onto her, wanted him to spin her around and devour her lips, but he didn't.

Orgasm blasted through her body suddenly, gripping around Gentry's finger in fast, hard pulses of pleasure. She grasped the back of his neck hard, digging her nails in as she whimpered his name.

Gentry pushed her forward fast, his hands strong and capable on her body, and before she knew it, she was bent over, legs locked and spread, hands splayed on the stone surface at knee-height in front of the fireplace. Behind her, the jingle of a belt sounded, directly followed by the quick snap of a button and rip of a zipper. Her orgasm pulsed on, even without his finger inside of her.

"Fuck," he muttered in a snarly voice. "You're not ready for this. Hell, I'm not ready. Blaire, you need to leave."

She should. She should've left before they had any intimacy, but she hadn't, and now she was in this, so worked up it was consuming her. "Are you going to take care of yourself when I'm gone?" She looked over her shoulder at him.

"Yeah," he answered gruffly. Gentry's sweater

was off, and his chiseled chest heaved with breath. His body was scarred, but tanned and smooth between what looked like slashes across his torso. His six-pack flexed with every breath, and his jeans were pushed gloriously low. The deep V of muscle led directly to his thick erection, swollen and ready. A wave of want took her, which was insane because she was still coming from what he'd done to her.

His eyes were such a bright green right now. He was beautiful. A beautiful, scarred-up creature who was clearly dangerous, but who made her feel completely at ease somehow. "Can I watch?" Heat flushed her cheeks at her brash question. "I-I've never watched, you know…before."

Gentry's blond brows winged up as he rested his hands on his hips. "You want to watch me get off." It wasn't a question but a semi-confused statement instead.

Mortified, Blaire stood suddenly and strode for the door. "Forget it. It was silly. I don't know what I'm talking about."

Her fingertips brushed the door handle, but she was spun around before she could wrench it open. Gentry's hand went around the back of her neck, and he pulled her to him. He leaned in fast. The second his lips touched hers, the fire in her body jacked up to magma-level heat. It was one part pain and two parts pleasure as she threw her arms around his neck and kissed him back. His lips moved against hers so skillfully she didn't have time for first-kiss jitters. She hadn't kissed anyone but her ex-husband since she was sixteen, but good grief, Gentry Striker was making this ridiculously easy on her. He was the leader, the aggressor. His hand clenched in her hair, and he turned her head where he wanted it, angled his face as his lips moved against hers. The man could kiss. Blaire stood there stunned at what was happening, at the insane reaction her body was having to him. He pulled away far enough to ease his jeans down his hips, and his bright white smile was nothing shy of wicked. And those dang eyes looked a completely different shade of green now. They were like the clearest ocean green, but with an inner glow that was striking in the soft light.

She reached for his shaft, but he shook his head slowly. "You said you wanted to watch. You want to help?" He flicked his gaze to her crotch, then back to her. "Let me watch you, too."

Oh, he looked like a bad boy right now. He locked one arm beside her head and pulled a slow stroke of his erection, eyes daring her to look down.

"But…the lights are on," she murmured.

His smile turned devilish in an instant. "Do you only touch yourself in the dark, Trouble?"

"Uh, yes. Doesn't everyone?"

He chuckled a deep, dark sound and leaned forward, sucked her neck hard. "No," he said against her neck before he eased back and pulled two more smooth strokes of his dick. "There's no shame in touching yourself."

Gentry was sexy as frick right now, pardon her French. He was dang near hypnotizing her with the way the head of his swollen cock pressed through the fist he made. He would feel so good inside of her. So big. Gosh, why did she feel so wild with him? This wasn't like her to fool around with a guy she had no chance at something long term with, but here she was, feeling utterly reckless and wanting everything from him before he closed down on her. And he would. He would close down tomorrow because that's what men did. But tonight, she wanted to shed her good girl cloak and be rebellious for once in her life.

With a squeak, she closed her eyes and slid her hand down the front of her pants.

"Eyes open, Trouble, or you'll miss it. You wanted the end, right? You want to watch me finish. You want to see the end because you pretend you're a clean girl, but deep down you like the mess."

Her cheeks burned as she pushed her finger into herself, but she did ease her eyes open.

"Stop making that face. Feels good to me, feels good to you. I think you look sexy as fuck taking care of yourself. You're teaching me the pace you like. Put on a good show so I know how to take care of you. Ffffuck," he said on a breath as his hips bucked.

Beside her, his hand made a fist against the door and his arm shook. He was trying to keep it together, trying to make her feel safe in this moment they were sharing, but it was getting him off. Sexy man.

His bicep flexed as he slid his hand up and down his shaft faster. He was right. There was no shame in them spending this moment together. They were both consenting adults, and he wasn't making her feel weird about this, so why should she? Plus, watching him do this was a huge turn-on. Maybe it was the sexiest thing she'd ever been a part of, and she didn't want to waste precious seconds of it on shame.

Blaire gripped his arm next to her face and rocked her head back as she matched his pace. There was something so intimate about doing this with Gentry, completely vulnerable, eyes locked on each other's, breath racing, connected in ways she didn't understand but didn't want to question right now.

"Fuck," he huffed out, pressing his forehead against hers. "I want to be inside of you so bad right now."

Okay. She shoved one side of her pants down, but he gripped her wrist and stopped her. "Don't, or I won't be able to stop myself. We can't do that. I'm not even supposed to kiss you."

"Wait, what?" she asked, trying to clear the fog from her mind. Not allowed to kiss her?

He grunted and shoved her shirt upward, exposing her breasts, and now the fog was back in her head but thicker.

"Watch," he growled out.

Blaire looked down in time to see him push into his hand, hips bucking and twitching, as creamy warmth streamed from the head of his cock and painted her stomach. He reared back and pushed into his fist again, and there was more warmth, and then more and more.

Between the focused look on his face as he stared hungrily at her breasts, and the way he was emptying himself onto her belly, this was the most erotic thing she'd ever witnessed.

It was so mind-numbingly hot, she had completely forgotten about taking care of herself, but Gentry pulled her hand away and then slid his hand into her panties again and pushed two fingers into her this time. He was slow and steady until he had her writhing against him. His lips pressed against hers, and he swallowed her moans as she came again.

Gentry smiled against her lips, and though she couldn't see it, only feel it, Blaire knew without a shadow of a doubt it was a cocky, wicked grin that would probably melt her panties all over again. With a spent sigh, she pushed her shirt down to her hips and sagged against him. Right about now, she felt like a noodle. A part of her expected Gentry to bolt, or push her out the door immediately. Matt wasn't a cuddler and escaped her as fast as possible after sex, but Gentry didn't seem to mind staying here in the moment. He held her so tenderly she didn't understand.

Slowly, she slid her arms around his shoulders and just stood there in his warm embrace, frowning at the flames in the hearth behind him and wondering if this was for real. Wondering if she hadn't just dreamed all of this.

Gentry, this almost-stranger, had just given her the single most beautiful and intimate experience, and now this rough-and-tumble, scarred-up, bright-eyed, bar-fighting, snarly man was holding her like she was as fragile as dandelion fluff. And was that his lips against the top of her head? She repaid him in kind by pressing a gentle kiss against the tripping pulse in his throat. His heart was pounding fast when she pressed her palm over the left side of his chest. She smiled and eased back so she could see his eyes, but he had them averted. And from this angle, they looked odd. Too bright, and his face was twisted up in a wild look she didn't understand. Perhaps it was a trick of the sconce lighting and flickering flames.

Gentry pulled her away from the door enough to open it, and oh, here was the sendoff. Disappointment unfurled in Blaire's chest. It had all been so beautiful while it lasted. He guided her with a gentle touch on her lower back. She half-expected him to say goodnight and go back in before she got off the porch, but he shocked her when he walked her silently the entire way to her cabin across the snowy parking lot. She was freezing again, on account of the blanket that was still sitting in the middle of his great room, the wetness on her stomach, and the frigid temperature, but he seemed perfectly at ease without a shirt on. His perfect little nipples weren't even perked up.

"You're not cold?" she asked.

He'd had a faraway expression in his face, but at her question, Gentry frowned and looked down at himself. "Oh. Uh, I'm used to living in cold temperatures. My body adjusted a long time ago." He zipped up his pants and fastened his belt like that would convince her.

"Right," she murmured suspiciously, stepping up onto her porch. "Well, thanks for dinner and, you know...after." At least her cheeks were warm.

Gentry stayed on the bottom step but still wouldn't look at her. He ran his hand roughly over his head. "I had fun."

Blaire pursed her lips at how detached he

sounded. “Me, too,” she murmured. “Night, Chaos.”

The corner of his lip quirked up, and he flashed her a bright-eyed look. “Night, Trouble.”

He turned and strode for his cabin, his hands shoved in his pockets, eyes on the woods to the left, and his breath freezing on every exhale.

She turned to go inside, but Gentry called over his shoulder, “Hey, Blaire?”

“Yeah?”

“If you’re into macaroni, it’s happening at eight in the morning before I head into town.” His wicked grin was back as he stood in the middle of the shadowy parking lot.

He was giving her a charming smirk that probably got him whatever he wanted with other women. Dangerous territory, that one.

Blaire leaned on the railing of her porch and played coy. “I’ll have to check my schedule.”

He narrowed his eyes and nodded. “Probably best if you’re busy. I’m bad news for a woman like you.”

“What kind of woman is that?” she asked, trying not to let her teeth chatter.

His grin slowly grew. “A good girl.” He gave her a

wink and turned, his gaze lingering on her for a moment before he gave her his back and walked to his cabin without another look.

Oh, that man knew what he was doing. He knew how to play games. For a moment, she'd thought she was the feline, but he'd reminded her she was the tiny mouse instead. He'd known the exact thing to say to dare her into joining him for breakfast. Call her a "good girl," and everything in her wanted to prove him wrong, especially after what they'd done tonight.

"Hmm," she hummed, narrowing her eyes as he closed the door to his cabin behind him.

She had the marrow-deep feeling that for the next week, Gentry Striker was going to be a beautiful distraction from the mess her life had become.

FIVE

What the fuck had possessed him to do that? He'd jizzed all over her like a dog marking his territory. And in a way, he was! His wolf thought that was a great idea, spraying her stomach like that. He hadn't meant to do it, though. He'd meant to keep her clean, but when it came down to it, she tasted so good, felt so warm and soft against his body, smelled so damn good, made those sexy little bedroom noises every time he touched her, he hadn't been able to stop his wolf. Shit! He couldn't lose control like that again. He'd been fighting his inner animal half the time they were fooling around. And he was letting his armor slip. She'd asked him about the cold not affecting him, but she hadn't bought his excuse. He could tell. Blaire was a smart woman. She would figure him out quick if he didn't get control of himself.

Kissing her? It was against werewolf law to mix with humans, and he hadn't even made it a damn night before he was on her like a rutting animal.

It wasn't supposed to be like this. Wolves didn't fool around with humans like he was doing with Blaire. She wasn't supposed to call to him, and yet here he was, pacing the living room, completely consumed by thoughts of her.

Okay. Settle down. There is a logical explanation.

Dad just died a week ago. Gentry was spiraling, in a place he hated, pissed at his brothers for staying MIA, and he was horny as fuck. Yeah, that was all this was. He would bring them back around to the friend zone tomorrow, keep his dick far away from her, and in six tiny days, she would be gone forever.

A long snarl blasted from his throat that he had to swallow down. He was breaking apart! Gentry needed to do something because pacing the living room wasn't helping, and he had another boner just thinking about the way Blaire's tits had looked all covered with his semen. God, he'd wanted her so bad. He'd wanted to be buried balls deep inside her more than he'd ever wanted anything. It was a miracle he didn't go too far. No, fuck that, he'd still gone too far. He'd kissed her and touched her and made her come twice, and then he'd freaking marked his territory like an animal. And she wasn't his! Not even close. Could never be his, so again, what the fuck was he doing?

He wanted to kill her ex for making her feel invisible, and he didn't even know the asshole. He wanted to feed her, and not macaroni like he'd joked. The first thing he'd done when he came back in was pull out a sirloin from the freezer to thaw because Blaire deserved steak and eggs and food fit for a queen. She was a queen. Classy but with a secret freak-side he found so damn sexy. Would probably make cute little red-headed pups. No, not pups—she was human. Something was wrong with him, or broken. And, hell yeah, he was panicking. He'd never even met another werewolf who hooked up with a human, and here he was imagining Blaire holding his firstborn kid. Fuck!

Gentry needed to Change.

His entire body was humming and felt like it was being shredded. This was going to suck with a healing rib, but there wasn't any help for it. He would never sleep until he let the wolf roam the winter woods outside.

He undressed on his way to the back door, leaving a pile of jeans and boxer briefs in his wake. Outside, the snow prickled against his bare feet, but it still wasn't uncomfortable enough to make him wince. He froze and listened. Blaire's soft voice was so quiet behind the walls of her cabin he could barely make out her humming. She was happy.

Good.

"Stop caring," he growled out to his asshole wolf. "You're going to get us killed."

And worse than that, he was going to get Blaire hunted. A relationship would be dangerous for both of them. Werewolves didn't go too far off the beaten path. Not even rogues paired up with humans. It was taboo. It wasn't just frowned upon either. It. Was. Forbidden.

Breeding with humans would be the end of the species. It would mean no more werewolf pups being born. It would mean exposure to other humans and certain death in some government testing facility somewhere, or as war-dog weapons in human wars.

There were rules in place for a reason, and Gentry believed in the need for those rules.

Bullshit.

"Fuck you."

His spine cracked, and Gentry bent in on himself suddenly. His wolf was punishing him by crippling his body and Changing slowly, breaking one bone at a time and drawing out the pain.

He gritted his teeth against the urge to grunt. That would only make Wolf happy. He hated when it was like this, when he and the animal were fighting. It was times like these that Gentry realized just how much control Wolf had.

Minutes of torture dragged on, but still Gentry refused to cry out. He wouldn't give Wolf the satisfaction, and the last thing he needed was for Blaire to come out and investigate a strange noise. He hadn't made it far enough away from the house and was breaking apart in the snow just on the edge of the back porch light.

Those minutes felt like an eternity, but at long last, the pain subsided, and Wolf lay panting and whole on a layer of ice. His fur kept him warm from the stiff wind, and he could smell everything, see everything, hear everything. Blaire was singing a bluesy song about a man falling from everything to nothing. She didn't sound unhappy, though, despite the song choice. Pretty voice. She would make a good she-wolf. Pretty howl. Too bad his bite wouldn't turn her. Only ten percent survived the bite, and most of them were men. His bite would poison her for three days until she passed away in a slow death that would turn any witness's hair gray.

He wasn't supposed to kiss her for a reason. Werewolves liked to bite when they fucked. The instinct had been there tonight, overwhelming almost. All it would take was one hard kiss, a bleeding lip just deep enough, and he would be the death of her. Fragile humans. Easily poisoned. Easily killed.

He couldn't be the death of her.

Wolf stood and shook snow from his coarse, gray coat.

He wouldn't hurt her. The woods blurred by as he loped through the thick trees and brush. He couldn't hurt her. She was his to protect from the Bone-Ripper Pack. At least for a week. He wouldn't bite her too hard. He would be gentle with her always if it meant he could keep her.

We can't keep her, Wolf. The human side of him was Logic.

But Wolf was Instinct. Wolf was Want and Desire. *Fuck you, Logic.*

He huffed a wolf laugh as the human side tried to Change back. It was a wave of nausea and then nothing. Logic thought he was in control, but he wasn't. Wolf only let him think that so he could function normally around the humans and blend in. Dumb fuck thought he was going to put Blaire in the friend-zone tomorrow. Hell no.

Wolf was going to hunt her down a present, and tomorrow he would fuck her proper. Get her attached to him. Make her crave him. Get her to love him and stick around. He'd wanted a mate for two years, and Logic had denied him. Logic had run from every woman, thinking they would settle him. He'd run from everyone and everything he'd ever known. He'd made them be rogues, but maybe Wolf didn't want to be a rogue anymore. Maybe he didn't want to be on the outside. Maybe he wanted everything. War, blood, pack, Blaire, pups from Blaire.

She won't make you pups, Wolf. She can't.

Wolf yipped to drown out the voice of his human side.

Wolf wouldn't let Logic run from Blaire. Perhaps he would hunt her ex and bleed him slowly so she wouldn't look sad anymore when she talked about him. She wasn't invisible. She was vibrant and beautiful and funny and everything good that Wolf wasn't. She would wash his soul clean. She would make him forget all the wolves he killed, all the bad things he'd done.

She would make him forget how much his heart hurt when he thought about Dad, Roman, and Asher.

Wolf was dark inside, always had been, but Blaire was bright and chased away the shadows. She made him want to breed and settle. She made him want to defend her and protect her and make her happy. She made him want to take care of someone other than himself, fight more efficiently, and claim territory.

Blaire Hayward—fragile human beauty—made him want to be a better werewolf.

SIX

Blaire held the comforter clutched to her chest as she listened to another long wolf howl rising. Rising like the sun on the eastern horizon, rising like the fine hairs all over her body.

She'd had no idea wolves lived in this area, but the terrifying predator had lifted his voice for the first time five minutes ago, and Blaire was still frozen in fear, even safe and warm inside the cabin.

It sounded so close.

It was probably just the mountains making the voice carry and sound much closer than it was. And see? There, it stopped now. The monster was probably on its way back to its den miles and miles and miles away to sleep for the day. She hoped. Blaire knew embarrassingly little about wolves.

As the minutes dragged on and the animal didn't sing again, a wave of potent relief washed through her. Sure, the sound had been beautiful, and a part of her felt lucky. How many people could say they'd heard a wild wolf howl? But animals with sharp teeth and hunting instincts scared her.

Blowing out a sigh to expel the rest of her tension, Blaire rolled out of bed and padded to the kitchen to put on a pot of coffee. But when she reached the main living area, a horrifying scratching sound shook the front door.

Blaire yelped and bolted the rest of the way to the kitchen, grabbed the biggest knife out of the block, and held it toward the door with shaking hands as another scratch rattled the door. It sounded like a dog clawing to get in, but in her heart, she just knew it was the wolf that had been making all that noise.

She was being hunted.

Her cell phone was in the bedroom on the charger. Maybe she should call the police, or animal control. Gentry would've been her first choice, but she didn't have his number, and she sure as heck wasn't opening a window to yell at his cabin. She didn't want to get her face eaten off by a freaking wolf!

She stood there petrified except for her shaking hands clutching the butcher knife. Her legs wouldn't move because in her illogical fear-filled mind, if she moved, the wolf would sense her in here like some heat-seeking dinosaur, break through the front window, and devour her.

Move, she mouthed to herself. As quietly as she could, she padded to the front window and pushed the curtain aside slowly with her fingertips.

There was something on the porch, but it wasn't the wolf she'd imagined.

It looked like a... Blaire narrowed her eyes. Was that a limp turkey?

Movement caught her eye, and she nearly swallowed her tongue when she saw Gentry headed this way over the snow-covered parking lot. He wore jeans low on his hips and was pulling a white sweater over his head. Abs and perfect chest and that sexy V of muscle and, holy moly, she'd forgotten for a moment how drop-dead gorgeous he was. But when his face showed through the neck hole, she grimaced and hunched her shoulders. He looked utterly pissed off. What had she done now?

He marched up the porch with a deep frown on his face, picked up the—yep, it was definitely a dead turkey—by the feet and stomped off the porch and back toward his cabin.

Blaire sprinted for the door, threw it open, and yelled out before he got too far away. "What just happened?"

"Nothing important," he called in a voice that was hoarse like he'd been yelling all night. "Breakfast is canceled. Rough night. I'll see you later." He didn't even turn around once before he made his way back into his cabin with the limp poultry and slammed the door behind him.

The wind was arctic against her cheeks, but the sting of the frigid temperature was nothing compared to the slap she felt on her heart. Last night she hadn't been able to sleep because she was so excited about breakfast. She was looking forward to seeing Gentry again and getting to know him better. A man who made her body feel like it did last night had to be worth getting to know, right? He hadn't just screwed her and fulfilled his own desires. He'd taken care of her, put her needs before his, made her come twice to his once, and didn't push them too far.

Too far…

Some dim memory ate at the very corner of her mind. *I'm not even supposed to kiss you.*

He'd said that last night, but distracted her away from the admission immediately. What did that mean?

Realization slammed into her like a sack of bricks. He wasn't supposed to kiss her because he was with someone. He didn't wear a wedding band. She'd checked. But that didn't mean he was single. Now it made sense. He was off the table, and look what they'd done.

Blaire felt sick to her stomach.

She didn't know who his girlfriend was, but Blaire's guilt was bottomless. And if she was honest, she was instantly mad at him for not telling her and not stopping them last night.

He was only the second man she'd experienced intimacy with, and now she'd probably ruined some poor girl's life who probably loved him, because why wouldn't she? Gentry was confident, mysterious, strong, and sensual, and now he was chopping dang logs in that sexy tight sweater and jeans like he was some sexier version of the abominable snowman. If she had a rock disguised as a snowball right now, she would chuck it at his dick. The dick he was supposed to be using on his girlfriend. Or crap, she could even be his fiancé, Blaire didn't know.

She slammed the door hard, but it banked back and hit her. With a screech, she slammed it again, followed it with her fists, and punched it closed the rest of the way.

"Ouch," she yelped, rubbing her knuckles. Her fury was still infinite, bubbling up inside of her until she couldn't see straight, so she stuck out her middle finger at the door. Felt good, so she did it with the other hand, too. And then she alternated her middle-fingers, jamming them toward where stupid, sexy Gentry was chopping wood like a dang hot lumberjack, probably to tempt her into being the other woman again. She made machine gun sounds as she punched her birds at the door. Still enraged, she karate kicked at the air, and then stomped into the bedroom.

She felt dirty. So *dirty*! This was all his fault. She might puke. *Don't look at the toilet.*

Blaire's eyes burned with tears that she refused to let spill, so she blinked over and over. She readied for the day in a haze, her mind spinning around and around her disappointment, not only in herself for not getting to know him better before fooling around with him, but for him being an unfaithful B-hole. And to be honest, her heart hurt way more than it should've. This was what men did, right? Of course, it was. Gentry was seven levels out of her league, younger than her by years, and the owner of this giant, beautiful inn. He could have whoever he wanted. And he did! And last night it just so happened to be her. Tonight it would be whoever he was dating.

She would not cry over this, not one single tear. This was part of getting back out there and dating. Ashlyn had warned her about this. She'd told her exactly how the dating world was, and Gentry had lived up to Ashlyn's warnings one hundred percent.

Lesson learned. Time to move on.

Only it wasn't so easy. She really, *really* liked him for reasons beyond her comprehension. The second she'd laid eyes on him, her body had liked him in some strange chemical reaction she hadn't had with anyone else, and then with every second she'd spent with him, her heart had liked him, too.

Of course he was freaking taken!

Today was a light make-up day, wild curls piled into a messy bun, skinny jeans, snow boots, a red sweater, and a thick winter jacket kind of day. No point in dressing up to attract that cheaty little cheater who was still chopping wood outside. *Chop, chop, chop*. It echoed through the house. Apparently, he had the stamina of a Clydesdale. Annoying.

Blaire grabbed her purse and left the house, trotted down the stairs, almost busted her butt on the icy bottom one, saved her balance, dusted off her jeans primly, and walked to her car, which was still parked in front of Gentry's cabin.

Gentry stopped slamming the ax into a wooden log, rested his hand on his hip, and leaned the handle onto the chopping block. His chest heaved with the exertion, his cheeks were slightly flushed under his facial scruff, and his breath chugged like fog in front of his face. "Where are you going?"

"None of your business."

"Uuuh, it is my business, remember? I said it wasn't a safe time in this town—"

Blaire held her hand up and cut him off. "Save your protective bullcrappery, Gentry. I don't need a controlling man in my life. You want to protect someone from imaginary monsters? Go protect your *girlfriend*!"

Was it mature to shout that last word, escape into her car, and slam the door? Nope, but it sure felt good to watch his face go slack.

She waved toodle-loo and then skidded to the exit of the parking lot like she was a stunt driver in a movie. At the stop sign, her tires spun out for a few seconds before they caught, but as soon as she got traction, she cast him a fiery glare and pulled out of Hunter Cove.

What was she up to this fine, blustery, gray-skied, frigid Maine day? Grocery shopping. She needed zero macaronis from Gentry Striker, and yes, that was a metaphor for his dick, too. Even if his dick was like…the biggest macaroni. A world record macaroni. *Stop thinking about how big it is.*

Blaire was an independent woman who didn't need a protector and sure didn't need anything from the man watching her leave.

Project avoid-the-heck-out-of-Gentry-for-the-rest-of-the-week started right now, because Blaire didn't need a hero.

She could take care of herself just fine.

SEVEN

How did one even cook an artichoke? Blaire spun the spikey thing in her hands. She would have to research. Or perhaps get mega-lazy and buy canned artichokes for the pasta she planned on making tonight.

She was an acquisitions editor for a big publisher, so she had a stack of manuscripts to read, a load of time on her hands, and a craving for carbs like she hadn't felt in months. Her appetite had been crap back home while stressing about work and Matt, but out here, she wanted to enjoy cooking and eating again.

This was going to be way better than the TV dinners she ate at the kitchen counter every night while staring pathetically at the two-person table she and Matt used to eat all their meals at together.

Tables were for families and couples. She'd held onto that old table so hard, but now she was considering selling it and replacing it with something that she picked out, not bought at a garage sale with her ex. Too many memories attached to it. Actually, there were too many memories attached to everything in that house.

Maybe it was finally time to sell it and rent something. A place she could build brand new memories away from Matt.

He'd moved on. It was way past time she did the same.

Relief and sadness welled up inside of her as she settled the artichoke in her cart and rolled it toward the pasta aisle.

She smiled at a couple as she passed, but they only frowned back at her, and the man snarled up his lip like a wild dog. Rude. The people in this store were either friendly or gave her looks like she was a leper. Now she was afraid to give anyone eye contact because the entire grocery store was apparently a mixed bag of nuts.

Gentry fit right in around here.

Blaire gritted her teeth hard to punish herself. She'd sworn not to think of Cheater-McGee while she was out and about running errands, but her mind kept circling back around like a little glutton for punishment.

Bowtie pasta or fettuccine? She scrolled through the recipe on her phone. She could do either. Blaire held up a bag of each and played eeny-meeny-miny-mo.

"I don't have a girlfriend."

The voice right by her ear startled her so hard she dropped the bowties on the floor and yelped.

She spun, and there was the man of her imaginings himself, now dressed in a green, threadbare V-neck sweater and sex-appeal. Her hormones were fangirling, and it made her even angrier.

"Fiancé then," she said sarcastically as she bent to pick up the pasta.

Only he bent over at the same time and reached for it, knocking into her shoulder. She went toppling backward. His strong arms gripped her wrists in a blur and settled her upright again so fast it stole her breath away.

He still held her wrists and was standing too close. He smelled like that body spray and mint, as if he'd just brushed his teeth, and this was the first time in her life she'd ever been jealous of a toothbrush. She hated everything. Blaire wrenched her wrists away from him and crossed her arms.

Gentry's eyebrow cocked up, and his lips curved slightly with a smile. "You're really cute when you're mad."

"I'm not cute. I'm a tornado. I'm an avalanche of fury."

Gentry pursed his lips, but he was doing a pretty crappy job of hiding his smile.

"Jerk," she muttered, tossing the fettuccini into her cart and motoring away from him. Only Daddy Longlegs could apparently speed walk and caught up with her in three strides. Obnoxious.

"Stalking is illegal, you know," she blurted out pertly.

"But you're so fun to stalk, Trouble. Jailtime would be worth it."

"Have you been arrested often?" she asked, lifting her chin and taking a left toward the wall of freezers. She was definitely loading up on pizza rolls.

"Have you?"

She tossed him an angry glare. "Of course not, I'm a good girl."

"I don't have a fiancé," he said low. I don't have a girl at all. I don't really know why you thought that. If I had someone who was mine, I wouldn't have been all over you last night. That's not me. It's not really possible for someone like me to…you know…"

"Cheat?"

"Yeah. I'm a one-woman kind of guy. Or…" Gentry's frown deepened. "I was really trying to be a zero-woman kind of guy. I'm shit at relationships."

"You don't say."

Gentry cast a quick glance around and pulled the cart to a stop. In a low voice, he murmured, "What are you angry about, Blaire? Explain it to me, because I have to tell you, women are a complete mystery to me, and you are the most confusing one of all."

She matched the low pitch of his voice because, apparently, they were telling secrets by the milk case. "I was looking forward to breakfast with you, Gentry. I thought maybe you were different than those guys who fooled around with a girl and bolted, but then first thing this morning, you throw attitude and cancel on me, and now I feel...I feel..."

"What?" he asked, looking utterly baffled. "Say it."

"I feel dirty and kind of cheap."

Gentry ran his hand over his head, pulling off his black winter hat, and blew out the word, "Fuck." He paced off then back and squared up to her even closer, trapped her in that bright green gaze. He lowered his voice again. "You aren't dirty and you aren't cheap. Last night wasn't just some screw-around for me, Blaire. It was scary. I'm not supposed to be with someone like you."

"Someone like me?"

"It's so fucking complicated right now. So complicated, and I don't want the hole I'm in to rub off on you, okay? I want you to have a good vacation, a good week. I want you to have good memories of this place." *Good memories of me.* The words were right there, unspoken but hanging in the air between them anyway.

Blaire was stunned with the honesty in his eyes.

"I didn't get any sleep last night, and I was moody and pissed at the damn wolf—" Gentry's eyes went wide as he cut himself off.

"You heard it, too? Gentry, it was terrifying! Howling right at dawn like that. I'll have nightmares for a week. I didn't even know there were wolves around here."

"Shhhh," he hissed, scanning the store around them. Quick as a whip, he grabbed the back of her neck and pulled her to him, settled his lips near her ear, and whispered, "There are a few newly released into the mountains, but it's a hot topic with the town. Best not to mention them."

"Okay," she murmured, feeling drunk on his smelly-good body spray. She was going to dress as his toothbrush next Halloween.

"Are you sniffing me, Trouble?" he asked, his lips brushing her ear.

No use denying it. "Mmm hmm." When Blaire clenched the fabric of his sweater in her fists, he reacted with a low, soft rattling noise in his throat that sounded wild and sexy.

"'Scuse me, love birds," a little elderly lady with thick glasses said.

Gentry backed away from Blaire like she was made of burning buffalo chips. He was pressed against her one second and on the other side of the cart the next, staring at the lady like they'd been caught boinking under the bleachers.

"Gentry," the woman said cheerfully.

"Nelda," he muttered, much less cheerfully. His eyes hardened like shards of green glass on the woman.

Blaire cast him a what-the-heck look and apologized to Nelda. "I'm so sorry."

"Don't be, dear, I used to act like that with my Ted. It's good to see young love again. Can you reach that for me?" She pointed at the two percent milk on the top shelf of the refrigerator.

"Of course," Blaire said, grabbing two, one for her and one for the nice lady.

Finally, someone with manners in this town.

"Thanks, sweetie." Nelda gave the brightest smile and then turned toward Gentry. In the softest, kindest voice Blaire had ever heard, she said, "She's pretty. Rhett's gonna kill you." And then she shuffled off, pushing her cart, humming under her breath. Oh good, another lunatic.

Blaire blinked slowly and shook her head to rid herself of that ruined moment.

Nelda wasn't sweet after all.

Nelda was a cock-blocker.

"I'm going to get some stuff for the house," Gentry said in a distracted voice as he watched the woman walk away through narrowed, angry eyes.

"Don't forget the macaroni," she joked.

Gentry huffed the softest laugh and then cast her a quick glance. He looked like he wanted to say something, shook his head hard, then strode off toward the front of the store.

Okay then. Blaire rubbed the edge of her ear softly just to remember what his lips had felt like there. Her body was still revved up, and right now, all she wanted to do was get lost in a hug from Gentry. He wasn't the public affection sort though, obviously, so she was barking up the wrong tree with wants like those.

Rhett's gonna kill you. What a strange thing to say. Wait, maybe Rhett was who Gentry got into a barfight with last night.

She frowned at where Gentry had disappeared and then pushed her cart toward the cartons of eggs stacked in an open refrigerator along the wall. She felt pulled in a hundred directions around Gentry. A part of her loved the excitement, but another part of her grew scared of all the mysteries that surrounded him. The more she thought she knew him, the more layers she found, and for the life of her, she couldn't figure out if she liked that about him or not.

One thing was for sure and for certain, though. Gentry Striker was going to keep her on her toes this week.

Thanks to him, her quiet vacation was getting more and more interesting by the minute.

EIGHT

Gentry rattled off a snarl as he followed Nelda's scent outside. Fucking snake in wolf's clothing would tell Rhett he was breeding a human before the old werewolf even pulled out of the parking lot. He needed to cut her off.

"Knew you'd come for me," Nelda bragged from where she leaned against the corner of the building.

Gentry gave a stiff smile to the human family walking past him and shrugged into his jacket for show as he settled beside her.

Nelda pushed up her glasses, which were a part of her disguise and she didn't need, onto her fluffy silver hair and bared her teeth. "What the fuck are you doing, pup? You're going to get us all found out."

"It's not what you think. She's here for a week on vacation, and then I'll never see her again."

Nelda was punching something onto her phone.

"What are you doing? Nelda, Rhett won't just kill me. He'll kill the human, too." God, he hated calling Blaire *the human*. She was so much more than that.

"I'm not texting Rhett, you dumbass."

"Then who?"

"Your brothers. Maybe they'll knock some sense into you."

"Well," Gentry said, leaning back against the brick wall beside her. "Good luck reaching them. I've been trying for days."

Nelda's phone beeped. "Roman said they're on their way."

Assholes.

"Look, I hate you—"

"Thanks," Gentry muttered.

"Everyone does—"

"Is there a point to this?"

"No, just thought you should know."

"Fantastic."

Nelda squinted up at him for a loaded moment, then sighed. "I know there was bad blood between your father and I, but that wasn't all my doing."

Gentry cast her a suspicious sideways glance. Nelda and Dad had always hated each other's guts. No female werewolf had ever given him so much trouble in his pack. "What do you mean?"

"I mean, he picked another. I was supposed to be alpha female. I was supposed to be his choice, and he didn't want me. I never forgave him. Still haven't. I'm glad the old coot's dead."

Nelda pushed off the wall and adopted her slower pace, settled her glasses back on her nose, and wandered toward the parking lot.

"But Dad never chose a mate," Gentry said, completely confused.

"That you know of," she answered without turning around.

What the fuck just happened? Nelda hadn't turned him in to Rhett, she'd contacted his brothers instead, and she'd just dropped this bomb on him. Nelda and Dad? There was an unsettling thought. He'd never met anyone more manipulative than Nelda until Rhett came along. He didn't blame Dad one bit for turning her down as his alpha female, but him choosing another? That had to be a lie. Gentry's mom had died when he and his brothers were so young, none of them even remembered her face, her voice, anything. As far as Gentry had known, Dad had decided not to take another mate after Mom passed. So what in the actual fuck was Nelda talking about?

There was a dark-headed woman sitting in an idling truck in the front handicap parking spot. Exhaust fumes plumed across the old brown truck, but it was the woman's direct gaze that held his attention. She had a round face, pitch-black eyes, and silver streaks in her long, black hair. Full lips, a wide nose, and delicately arched eyebrows. She was in her fifties, or early sixties perhaps. A real looker, exotic, and somehow familiar.

Chills rippled up his spine, and some long buried instinct told him to run.

Wolf didn't like that and growled for him to posture.

When Gentry stepped away from the building and straightened to his full height, the woman pulled out of the parking spot and drove away, but he could see her gaze flick to him in the rearview mirror.

"Gentry?" Blaire asked. She stood behind her cart of grocery bags with a concerned look in her pretty green eyes. “Are you okay?”

Wolf’s snarl settled, and he grew quiet, watching her. Gentry had trouble taking his eyes off her to check the direction the brown truck took out of the parking lot. “I’m fine. I just thought I saw someone I used to know.” Or…something. The sense of déjà vu was so overwhelming he could almost see the woman’s face, twenty years younger, right there at the edge of his mind.

“You look like you’ve seen a ghost,” Blaire said from right beside him.

God, he wished he could drape his arm over her shoulder right now. He wished he could tell the world he liked her, and that she was his to protect. He wished he could wrap her in a hug until the worry left her voice. He wished he could kiss her lips until the little wrinkles of concern smoothed from her forehead.

Instead, he forced a smile and shoved his hands into his pockets to curb the urge to touch her. “I’m fine. Come on. I have some more errands to run in town, but I can load up your groceries for you.”

“Maybe I don’t need the help,” she challenged him.

Gentry chuckled. "And I like that about you. Fine, I'll stand back and stare at your ass while you unload the groceries into your car. Better?"

Blaire snorted the cutest little sound and bumped his shoulder as she pushed the cart beside him.

Beautiful girl. Her red curls were piled up high and messy. Made him want to pull the hair band out and fuck her on her back so he could mess it up. She wore hardly any of the make-up she had on yesterday so he could see her freckles. He liked them. She'd put some kind of mango-scented lip gloss on her full lips that he wanted to suck off, and when she turned her head to check if cars were coming, he spied a tiny red heart tattoo right behind her ear.

Blaire wasn't the good girl she claimed to be. She had some bad girl in her, too. Fucking sexy little tattoo that probably stayed hidden most of the time. He wanted to kiss it and make her let off that soft moan she had when he'd whispered up against her ear in the store. She'd been so wet for him last night. He could smell her pheromones now. She was probably soaking her panties for him, and all he'd done was stand close to her. Good Blaire, reacting to him the way he needed her to.

"Have you heard a word I've said?" she asked, arching her ruddy brows at him.

"No," he said honestly. "I was thinking about last night."

Blaire jerked upright, and her cheeks instantly colored with the prettiest pink he'd ever seen. "Dirty stuffs?" she asked innocently.

"Yep."

"You swear you don't have a girlfriend before we continue this conversation."

Gentry chuckled darkly. "Trouble, no woman has ever been willing to put up with my shit. You're free and clear to chase me." What was he doing? He shouldn't be encouraging the flirting, but he couldn't help himself. She was so damn fun to mess with, and that sexy blush was staining her cheeks even darker now. It made him want to say filthy things to her.

"I chased a man once, and it didn't work out so well."

"Your ex?" he asked, trying for nonchalance, but his fists clenched up in his pockets with the urge to choke the shithead who hurt her.

"Yep. I've realized chasing men isn't for me.

Maybe this time I want to be chased."

The vision of her as a pretty white rabbit and him as a big bad wolf flashed across his mind. If she knew what kind of monster he was, she would never say things like that.

Blaire popped the trunk of her rental car, and as tempting as it was for him to stand back and perv-watch how her ass pressed against her tight jeans, he couldn't let her work alone. Instinct wouldn't allow it, so he helped, then shut the trunk when they were done. "Get in the car and turn the heater on. I'll get rid of the cart."

Her eyes got all mushy like he'd done something heroic, and Gentry couldn't help the smile that took his face as he pushed the cart into the line with the others. He really liked making her happy. He also liked that she was easily pleased. Blaire suited him.

He jogged back over to her car, scanning the parking lot for any prying eyes because he couldn't stand the thought of not saying goodbye for some reason. He shouldn't do this. It was dangerous and could get them both hurt, but Gentry couldn't stop the urge to touch her.

So he leaned into the open window, kissed her,

pushed his tongue into her mouth in a single stroke just to taste her, then sucked on her lip hard and eased out of her car. It was a second of intimacy, but the stunned smile on her lips made it worth the risk.

"See you in Hunter Cove," he said through a smirk as he stepped back.

Blaire was just sitting there, touching her lips with her fingertips, staring at him with those pretty green eyes. "Okay. Thank you."

Thank you? Gentry's smirk deepened to a Grinch smile. He'd kissed her into shock or something. God, he'd never wanted a woman like he wanted her. Trouble, trouble, trouble.

He shoved his hands in his pockets as she eased out of the parking spot, and then just like at the cabin when she'd driven away from him, Gentry watched her go until he couldn't see her anymore.

Inside of him, Wolf howled to go after her.

Blaire didn't have to worry. She was definitely going to be chased.

NINE

Blaire flipped the page over and began reading the next. This manuscript was rough, but she was really trying to stick with it through chapter three at least to give the author a chance to find her stride. Blaire had been an acquisitions editor for years but had only found a couple of breakout authors. Her boss called her "too picky in this market," but the only thing that kept her motivated to keep going at this career was the idea that there was some unknown author out there with a hidden brilliance who just needed a shot. She wanted to be a part of a career like that. She wanted to be the one to breathe life into that first manuscript and help push the author onto the first leg of their journey to the top of the mountain.

The studly studmuffin laved his lick-pad up her stomach, and pumped his fishing rod faster into her tackle box. Suddenly he howled out her name as his baby gravy sprayed into her echoing treasure cavern…

Nope. Blaire slammed the first couple of chapters back on top of that horrifying page in a desperate attempt to evict the words "baby gravy" from her mind for eternity. She'd had high hopes about this one, but once again, she would be sending a rejection letter. That was the downside to her job. She was a dream-crusher to many in her quest to be a dream-maker for one.

She heaved a sigh and stared out the window again. Gentry had been gone all day. She'd had all these plans to make dinner, entice him over with the rich smell of pasta, and then possibly seduce him because, despite the fishing rod reference her poor mind had just been exposed to, she was in a constant state of arousal.

That would be one Gentry Striker's fault.

But he'd been MIA, and she'd had a vacation

dinner for one and a big glass of wine. Before she'd left home, Blaire had printed out a dozen manuscripts thinking it would be romantic to read actual paper books while on her snowy vacation, but she didn't feel like working tonight. She felt like more kisses, like the one Gentry had surprised her with in the grocery store parking lot.

She couldn't stop thinking about it, couldn't stop touching her lips and imagining the way his mouth felt and tasted. The way his short facial scruff felt against her soft skin, or the way her stomach did flip-flops when Gentry had pushed his tongue past her lips.

She hadn't been kissed like that in...well...ever. The way she was with Gentry couldn't be compared to anyone else, not even Matt.

Her phone lit up and vibrated against the counter in front of her. Ashlyn's name came across the caller ID, and Blaire smiled as she answered. "Yes, I'm still alive, no I didn't get lost for long, and no, I'm not working. Anymore."

"Ew, Hayward, please tell me you didn't bring manuscripts with you on freaking vacation."

"I can't help it. I left for this trip last minute, and I

wasn't caught up. I have deadlines, you know."

Ashlyn made a gagging sound.

"I do have something that will make you happy, though."

"Good, my day sucked balls. I need good news."

"Wait, what happened?"

"Gary from the office downstairs asked me out again."

"Butt-grab Gary?"

"Yes, he won't take no for an answer, and I got stuck, literally stuck, in the elevator with him this afternoon. I'm pretty sure he was the one who pulled the alarm. He tried to kiss me. I almost pepper-sprayed him."

"Ash, it's time to go to HR about him."

"Yeah I know, but I hate being a whiny rat. I wanted to handle it on my own and just be done with it. Tell me good news so I can stop imagining his fish lips coming at my face."

"Okay, okay, guess who I called a little while ago?"

"I swear to God if you say Matt, I'm going to reach through the phone and give you two purple nurples."

Blaire covered her nipples protectively on instinct. Ashlyn didn't bluff about that stuff. "No! I called that realtor you told me about. Andrew."

Ashlyn gasped really loud into the phone. "Say it fast, Hayward."

"I'm putting the house on the market."

Ashlyn crowed like a rooster so loud Blaire had to pull away the phone. "Finally ladies and gents, she is moving on from Matt the Chode!"

"Don't call him that. He was family for a long time, and he wasn't so bad."

"Cough, cough, bullshit, you are too forgiving. You should move to my apartment complex. We can be neighbors."

Blaire giggled and leaned her elbows on the counter. "I haven't thought about where I want to live yet, but I'll start looking when I get back."

In a softer voice, Ashlyn said, "I knew this vacation would be good for you. I just had this feeling when I was looking for cabins that this one was special. And look. Day one of getting out of here and out of that damn house you used to share with him, and you already sound so much happier."

And here was the moment. It was the moment

she was supposed to tell Ashlyn about Gentry because, really, he could be credited with starting the change in her. Oh, she had no grand illusions about them ending up a couple and having a hundred babies and growing old together, but he'd made her realize something pivotal. She wasn't dead, and neither was her heart. And holding on to Matt would only hurt possible relationships in the future. Gentry made her want better. He made her want companionship again, flirting, sex, affection, having someone be there to ask how her day was, and her listen to their day in return. She wanted someone to eat meals with, and that wasn't going to happen in a house full of the ghost of her broken marriage.

But right as she parted her lips to tell Ashlyn about the man who was creating big changes in her heart, headlights arced across the front window, and the *studly studmuffin* himself was home.

A huge swell of relief filled her. It was as if she'd released a breath she hadn't known she was holding. Maybe it was from him coming home last night all beat up, and she was worried. Or perhaps a little piece of her thought he would bolt and not come back until her vacation was finished. He'd been upfront with his urge to roam.

"Hey, I have to go," Ashlyn said. "My mom has called three times, so it must be important. I'll talk to you tomorrow. No working!"

"I'll try not to."

"And take lots of pictures and send them to me so I can live vicariously through you while I karate chop Gary's kisses away."

Blaire snorted. "Okay deal, I'll send you snow pictures tomorrow. It's beautiful up here. There's even a wolf."

"Oh, get pictures of the wolf. I want that, too. Gah, Mom is calling again. She's probably on Web MD freaking herself out."

"Tell her I said hi."

"Will do, bye-bye now."

Blaire ended the call and grinned big when a knock sounded at the door. She really liked that he came to see her before he even went into his house.

When she opened the door, he stood there in an unbuttoned tan winter jacket and tight V-neck sweater, exposing the top of the perfect line between his pecs. His winter hat was pulled low, but it's dark color made his green eyes look even brighter. Arms locked against the door frame, he canted his head and gave her a crooked smile that made her ovaries go boom.

"I got you a birthday present," he said in that sexy, deep rumble of his.

"Is it...something dirty?" she asked hopefully.

"Oh, it's filthy." His smile stretched wider, and inside, her inner sex goddess bounced and clapped like a seal.

Gentry pulled something from his back pocket and handed it to her.

It was a paintbrush.

"Filthy, huh?" she asked in a dead voice.

"Oh, we'll have paint all over the place," he said in a phone-sex operator voice. His smile was obnoxious.

Blaire crossed her arms over her chest. "Perhaps I don't want to spend my second night of vacation painting."

The smile dipped from his lips as he pushed off the door frame. He shifted his weight and looked off into the woods. "Painting isn't the point."

"What is?"

He leveled her with a look. "Spending time with

me."

She inhaled sharply at what he did to her heartbeat. "Is this...is this like a painting *date*?"

"I don't date." When a soft sound came from his chest, he shook his head hard. "I can't, but I want to spend time with you. I have a million things to do around here to get it fixed up to sell, but you're only here for six more days, and I don't want to waste our time together."

She really liked the way he'd said *our time*.

Slowly, she took the paintbrush from his hand and ran her fingers across the soft bristles. "Let me get dressed in some old clothes, and I'll be right out."

Standing aside, she nodded her head for him to come in and hoped to God it was as smooth as she'd tried to make it. Gentry was really good at winks, head nods, and smexiness, while she still felt like an amateur with this flirting stuff.

Gentry strode in with the smooth gait of a lion as he stripped out of his jacket. She made a beeline for the bedroom so she could get dressed in a rush and stare at him again that much faster.

"Wear something warm," he called from the other room.

"You're telling me to put more clothes on?" Blaire stared into her drawer of old night shirts and pouted.

"Or you can wear nothing," he suggested. "I'll be happy, but you'll freeze your perfect little ass off."

"I like that you called my ass little, ya liar."

A deep chuckle sounded from the other room, and then, "You read books?" The soft noise of paper rustled, and she imagined him skimming the manuscript that was sitting on the counter.

"Yeah, lots of them. Read page eighteen."

More papers rustled as Blaire pulled her hair into a high ponytail, and then Gentry huffed a laugh. "Baby gravy?"

Blaire giggled and shoved her legs into a pair of leggings with a hole where her inner thighs had rubbed it threadbare. She called these her "easy access pants," but Gentry didn't need to know that. "I'm an acquisitions editor for a publisher. I read a lot of manuscripts and pick the ones to bring to my boss. I try to get the good ones contracts so they can distribute through the publisher I work for. Contracts, editing, marketing...there is an entire machine in my office. I'm just the first cog."

"Do you read paranormal romance?" he asked.

His tone had gone serious and dark, so she pulled on the black, thigh-length tunic sweater she'd bought on clearance for four dollars and poked her head out of the room.

"Like vampires? Nope, not my department, though I wouldn't mind reading something different. I mostly consider contemporary romances right now. Sometimes I look at motorcycle club romances if I'm getting antsy for a change, but then I'm right back on contemporary." She sat on the floor next to the door and shoved her feet into her snow boots. Distractedly, she admitted, "I used to love to read. It was my passion, and I thought this would be the perfect job for me. But it's different when you do your passion for a corporate setting, you know? Now reading is work, and I don't read the books I want to anymore, just the ones the publisher thinks will sell in the current market."

"Why don't you read outside of work?"

"Because I'm exhausted. I was overdoing it, overworking myself, bringing my work home, obsessing with staying distracted after my marriage fell apart, and I just...I don't know...lost the passion for reading a good book outside of work. It's like, if I have any extra time outside of the office, I don't want to be doing something that reminds me of my career anymore. It's the part I miss most, getting lost in a story that I don't have to pull out of to think about the plot, characters, believability, and whether my boss will go for the book or not."

Gentry was bent over the counter, fidgeting with the corner of one of the pages, his eyes trained on her tight-clad legs. "How many manuscripts did you print out for this week?"

"Twelve."

"Where are they?"

"My room," she muttered, tying her laces.

Gentry strode into her room and returned shockingly fast with her work satchel. "You can print these out again?"

"Yeah, they're saved on my computer," she murmured, following his progress toward the fireplace with her gaze. "What are you doing?"

"Freeing you up to actually take time off."

He dumped the manuscripts into the hearth and reached for a box of matches on the mantel.

A part of her revolted at the idea of burning

manuscripts, but as the flames caught on the edges, she thought perhaps Gentry had a point. If they were in the house, she would work this week, and it would take away from the time she had off.

"My best friend would like you," she murmured, drawing her knees up and watching the fire build. "She didn't want me to work this week either."

"The one who booked you this vacation?"

"Yeah. Ashlyn. She kept me sane the last few years."

Gentry leaned against the mantle, his back to her as he said, "She wouldn't like me for you if she knew me, Trouble." Then he cast her a quick, blazing-eyed glance over his shoulder and straightened his spine. With a plastered smile, he asked, "Are you ready?"

"Do I look like cat woman?" she asked, standing and dusting her bottom off. Her all-black skintight outfit was the oldest she had, but she also cared about being cute for Gentry. He looked like a runway model, and right about now, she looked like a starless night in a pushup bra, who was sporting some seriously obvious panty-lines.

He huffed a laugh and shook his head. "Trouble, you don't want to be a cat around me. You look sexy as fuck, though."

She gave him a cheeky grin. "Then yes, I'm ready right meow."

Gentry chuckled and rushed her, picked her up with his forearms resting right under her butt cheeks. "Oh, right meow?"

Blaire let off a little hiss and gripped her claws into the back of his neck.

"Retract those claws, kitty cat, or you'll be asking to get fucked against the table over there." Gentry's voice had gone silken, filled with promise.

The smile fell from her face. Whoa, he was good at putting hot images into her head. Her, naked, boobs down on the table, legs locked and splayed. Him driving deep inside her, hard, his face focused as he gritted out her name, his powerful body flexing with every thrust...

Gentry's nostrils flared slightly, and the expression on his face turned serious. He settled her on her feet and backed off. He wouldn't look her in the eyes anymore. "Come on, Trouble. We have to travel to get where we're going."

Blaire was still unstable, swaying slightly, and all her brain cells were currently focused on the churning sensation low in her belly. "Wait, what? I thought we were fixing up the cabins."

"We are and we aren't. I'll explain on the way." He plucked her thick winter jacket off the coatrack by the door and held it out for her, waiting.

It was hard keeping up with his mood swings, but she accepted his help with her coat and then pulled on her gloves. Now she was good and ready for the short trip to the truck.

He led her out the door and down the stairs.

"Geez, overprotective," she teased light-heartedly to lift the tension between them. "We're just going to the truck."

"False, we're hiking."

"Hiking?" Blaire blurted, her breath frozen in front of her face. "It's freezing out here."

Gentry didn't say anything as he led her to a wide trail through the woods. There were tire tracks, so why the heck were they walking at nine o'clock at night? "Um, a wolf lives out here," she reminded him, looking back longingly at the safety of the cabin. She'd left the main light on, and the soft glow was beckoning her back.

"You're safe with me," Gentry said without

turning around.

He was hard to keep up with, though, and even with the traction of her snow boots, she was slipping on the layer of ice beneath the snow, but Gentry didn't seem inclined to wait for her. Whatever survival-of-the-fittest nonsense he was pulling, she wasn't playing.

Bending down, she scooped up a big handful of snow, packed it tight, and chucked it at him. When the snowball exploded against the back of his jacket, Gentry froze like a gargoyle.

He turned slowly, his eyes narrowed to little, green slits.

"I used to play softball. I was pretty good," she bragged with a curtsy.

When Gentry stalked closer to her, bending smoothly to pick up snow, the cocky grin fell from her lips. "No, I was just playing. I just wanted attention!"

"You got it. You have all of my attention, Trouble. Why are you running?"

With a squeal, she high-kneed it off the trail and headed for the cover of the trees. A snowball hit her in the side, and she burst out laughing and made one of her own. He was jogging parallel to her through the trees. He looked like he belonged in these woods, while she was tripping on hidden tree roots every three steps or so. The forest echoed with their laughter as they chucked snow at each other and ducked behind trees. Gentry was fast, almost unnaturally so. One second he was twenty yards away, and the next he appeared from behind the towering maple tree she was about to hide behind as if he'd been there all along. With a remorseless grin, he plopped snow on top of her hair.

She gasped at the frigid sensation that trembled down her spine. "Gentry!" she exclaimed breathlessly.

"Mmmm," he said, more of a rumble than a word. "I like when you say my name like that.

"Like what? Angrily?" she screeched, scooping more snow.

He stood there in the moonlight, legs splayed, dick huge and pressed against his jeans, with the most confident smile she'd ever seen on anyone. "Apparently, I find anger sexy."

"That's not how it's supposed to work, Gentry!"

When she pelted him with a snow ball, he flinched but didn't flee. He was laughing instead.

The snowball fight clearly over, she tossed him a

fiery glare, which she was trying to hold because his smiles made her want to smile for some irritating reason.

"You still mad?" he asked from right behind her where he pressed his body against her back. His hand was in her snow-speckled hair, angling her neck to the side to give him access to suck her hard there, and ooooh, that felt so freaking good.

"Do you forgive me?" he murmured against her sensitive skin.

She'd never wanted a hickey in her life, but suddenly, she wanted one from Gentry more than anything in the world.

"No," she said on a breath.

Gentry turned her in his arms and walked her backward, slowly, gripping the back of her neck with one hand and resting his other securely on her hip.

When her back hit a tree, Gentry turned her face and kissed her right behind her ear, right where she'd gotten a little heart tattoo at age eighteen when she had one of her only moments of rebellion.

"I've wanted to kiss that little fucking heart all day," he whispered against her ear. "Has anyone kissed it before?"

"No," she uttered helplessly. Why were her legs going numb?

"Good. It's all mine then." He kissed it again, let his lips linger, then dipped his affection to her neck. "Do you forgive me now?"

Blaire blinked slowly at the full moon through the bare tree branches above. "No?" The word came out soft, like a question. Why? Because it was a huge lie. He'd basically kissed her into a coma without even touching her lips, and he was now forgiven for everything he had done and everything he would do again.

Gentry's chuckle was deep and resonated through his chest. He hadn't put his jacket back on, and her hand was splayed over the perfect line between his defined pecs. She could feel his laugh, but not well enough, so she pulled off her glove with her teeth and let it drop to the snow beside them. And then she slid her hand under the hem of his shirt. He twitched and then punched out a slight breath when her fingers brushed the lowest of his abs.

Her hands were cold, while Gentry felt like he was running a fever. A sliver of worry washed through her. "Are you okay?" Maybe he was coming down with a cold or something.

Gentry responded by pressing his hips against hers and guiding her wrist up higher under his shirt. "Never been better, Trouble. Now you're earning my forgiveness, too."

"Your forgiveness," she snorted.

"Who threw the first snowball?"

"Oh."

His abs were like mounds of stone, but his skin was smooth and soft. Up, up, she pressed on, memorizing his body until she reached his chest. And there, he splayed her palm against his pec, right over his pounding heart. His breathing was deeper, his cheeks flushed, and his erection was so hard against her she forgot the cold completely. It was so easy to get lost in moments like these with a man like Gentry. No, not a man like Gentry. Just Gentry. She'd never felt so consumed by another person in her entire life. It was terrifying and beautiful all at once.

"Can I tell you something?" he murmured, trapping her in that bright green gaze.

"You can tell me anything." And she meant it. She wanted to know everything about this man who was pulling yet another of her heartstrings onto him.

"I'm taking you someplace that's really special to me, to my family, and it used to be special to the people of this town. It's called Winter's Edge."

Chills blasted up her arms, but it wasn't from the cold. The way he'd said Winter's Edge, so reverently, made her realize just how special the paintbrush gift had been. He was showing her a big part of himself tonight. Gentry was letting her in.

"What is it?" she whispered.

His heart pounded faster under her palm, and he gripped her hips. "It's a bar. My dad left the place to me in his will. I haven't been back to this town in years, but I have good memories. Some, anyway. Winter's Edge is one of them. I grew up playing there, learning the business, working there when I was old enough. It was supposed to be mine."

"Like the inn?"

"The inn is secondary income. My dad didn't even make enough to float us on rentals at the inn, but Winter's Edge was where everyone used to hang out."

"What happened to it?"

"My dad died."

"When?" she whispered.

Gentry scrubbed his hand down his face and swallowed hard before he answered. "A week and a half ago."

"Gentry," she drawled out, her heart breaking for him. Blaire didn't know what possessed her to do it, but she stood up on her tiptoes and rested her cheek against his. They weren't hugging, just standing there, touching faces, both of their breath shaking in the silence of the night.

There were no words that she could say to make this easier on him, so she waited. And waited. And when he finally did pull her into a tight hug, she did her best to blink back the moisture that rimmed her eyes. She couldn't even imagine losing her mom. A week and a half? It had just barely happened, and Gentry had been walking around with all this pain, seemingly normal, and now she was starting to get a glimpse of just how strong Gentry Striker was. Not just physically—that had been apparent from day one. But he was strong emotionally in ways she truly respected.

"I went to Winter's Edge earlier to see if it needed repairs. I didn't think it would need anything, my dad loved that bar more than anything, but when

I went inside, it looked like no one had been in there for years. And I don't know what the fuck is going on in this town, Blaire. I came back, and nothing's what I thought it was. I talked to my dad on the phone all the time, and he'd acted like it was business as usual, told me the bar was doing fine. But the inn is so far underwater, the bar hasn't seen customers in God-knows-how-long, and I just want to leave and go back to my life, but I can *feel* it. I'm getting sucked in to whatever shit went down in Rangeley."

"Is it dangerous to dig?" she whispered.

"Yeah."

"Is that why you got in that fight last night?" she asked.

When Gentry released her and eased back a couple paces, she could see it in his eyes. The shut-down was here. "I've said way too much. More than I'm allowed. More than is safe. Come on," he said low, offering his hand.

Her palm tingled from being suddenly detached from his warm chest, but he was offering her what he could. He had to shut down on her for whatever reason, but he was still allowing her touch, which after that intimate moment of sharing, she really needed.

So she smiled sadly and slid her palm against his, stooped to pick up her glove, then shoved it in her back pocket with the paintbrush.

They'd gone from laughter with the snowball fight, to molten lust, to having a huge, illuminating experience in the matter of half an hour. And truth be told, Blaire was stunned with the amount of emotion this man brought out in her. She felt alive again. She wasn't just some ghost walking through her life waiting on the next day that would be the exact same as the one before.

For the first time, she dreaded going back to her life. It would mean back to the monotony, back to avoiding Matt in their hometown, back to trying to get on her feet. While here, she already felt upright.

But worst of all, in six tiny days, she would have to say goodbye to the man who was breathing life into her again.

TEN

The door creaked loudly as Gentry shoved it open. There was a pile of debris on the other side, keeping it from sliding easily, but he placed his thick-soled boot in front of it and made room for Blaire to go in.

"What's that smell?" she asked, covering her nose.

"Raccoon."

"Living?"

"Not anymore."

Geez, she didn't even want to know. It was so dark she could only make out the shadows of overturned tables and chairs.

When Gentry stepped out of the way of the door,

it slammed closed, startling her. “Follow me,” he said.

Blaire held her hands out, searching for him or a wall or a freaking walking stick, anything. “Wait, I can’t see to follow you.”

In no time flat, Gentry had pulled her onto his back like a little monkey, and she giggled at how helpless she must seem because, apparently, Gentry had impeccable night vision. He didn’t bump a single piece of furniture on his way to the back of the bar.

He settled her on a chair that made her sneeze with the amount of dust, and then one at a time, he lit four old-fashioned lanterns on the bar top. “I’ll get the power turned back on to this place tomorrow. Someone cut the lines.”

What the hell was going on in this town? And what was Gentry’s father involved in before he died that got him targeted like this?

The lanterns made a world of difference once Gentry and Blaire righted tables and settled the lights on them throughout the room.

Blaire stood in the middle of the cluttered area, and her heart ached for Gentry all over again. He wore a business, get-crap-done face as he upended chairs and stacked them against the side wall, but he'd said this place meant something to him, and there was no way seeing an old haunt torn up like this didn't hurt.

Determined, she gave a silent promise that he wouldn't have to clean this place up alone. For the next six days, she would help. Something deep down inside told her Gentry needed this place to be okay again for his father's memory.

Blaire checked her phone, which thankfully got a signal in here, and turned on her favorite playlist. And while the music was going, she and Gentry went to work. There were clean rags and cleaning solution in a case behind the bar, so she scrubbed the layers of dust off the bar and disinfected everything behind it until her arms shook. There wasn't a single bottle of liquor left in the cabinets that lined the wall behind the counter, but on the floor were piles and piles of glass. Someone must've been sending a mighty big message to break all this expensive liquor instead of stealing it. She swept the shards into a big orange bucket, and then went to sweeping the rest of the bar as well, which took long enough that Gentry had patched and painted a shredded wall by the time she was done.

He'd apparently picked up supplies, because the area near a small stage was stacked with sheetrock, nails, tools, paint, drop clothes, caulk guns, and more cleaners. There was even a sander for the wood floors as though he meant to re-stain them, and when she looked at the wooden boards closer, she could see why. Someone had broken out a few of the windows, and the weather had gotten to the floors. Pity, because they were probably originals.

"I don't know if they can be saved, but I don't really have the money to replace them right now," Gentry said, as if he could read her mind.

"Well, they already look a little better now that they're clean," she said hopefully.

"You know that little cabin beside yours?"

"The dilapidated one?" she said, pulling the paintbrush from her back pocket. It was getting really late, and she was tired, but she wouldn't stop until he did. Gentry needed this.

"Yeah, that's my favorite cabin on the property."

Blaire scrunched up her nose. "Really?"

"My dad never got around to rehabbing it, so it got rented the least during the busy season. So me and my brothers would hang out there sometimes. It was like our clubhouse."

"How many brothers do you have?"

"Two."

Blaire frowned. "Did they come to your dad's funeral?" AKA—why the heck weren't they here helping fix up his father's place?

"No. I'm waiting on them to spread his ashes."

"Are you the oldest?"

"I feel like it sometimes, but no. I'm the middle. My brother Asher is older by a year, and Roman is younger than me by a year."

"Busy mom."

Gentry handed her a cup of dark brown paint and smoothed out the drop cloth under him with the toe of his boot. "My parents wanted a lot of kids. Dad came from a big family and wanted the same. He wanted me and all my siblings to always have someone to depend on."

"Like a pack of Strikers," she teased.

But Gentry jerked a startled gaze to her, the smile gone from his face. "What do you mean?"

Blaire frowned. "Why are you being weird? I mean like a hoard of you. A gaggle. A herd? I dunno, pack just felt right for the joke."

The corners of Gentry's eyes tightened as he gave his attention to dragging his paintbrush down the corner line again. One of the lanterns was running low on fuel and flickered a bit, casting his face into shadows. She was staring, but couldn't help herself. His profile was perfect.

He licked his lips like she'd seen once on a cologne commercial, then cast her a quick glance. His eyes churned with something hungry. "You like what you see, Trouble?"

"Yep," she said honestly.

His lips curled back in a feral smile that somehow looked right on his face. Gentry was a wild man. She could see little peeks of it in the way he carried himself, the way he walked, and the way he didn't favor his injuries from yesterday. She could tell from the wicked glint in his eyes and the way his nose twitched like an animal when he was riled. Like now.

"You smell good," he said, his voice low and gravelly.

"Like mango? It's the lip gloss."

"Like mango and more."

She frowned. "Shampoo? Deodorant?" He must have a very good sense of smell for those things.

"Dangerous little kitty," he murmured, pulling her in front of him and pressing her back against the wall. "You make me want to tell you things."

"My deodorant is called powder fresh. Does that give you a boner?" she teased.

"It's not your deodorant I care about right now, Trouble."

He cupped her sex, and her response was an instant bowing of her back against the wall. She inhaled sharply.

Gentry pressed a fingertip into the 'easy access' hole like a little poontang-seeking missile. "I like the smell here better. I can tell when you want me."

"All the time," she murmured mindlessly.

"I can tell," he rumbled, teasing her with his lips. "Makes me want to eat you, kitty."

Chills rippled across her skin, raising the fine hairs all over her body. The way he'd said that... It was one part threat, two parts pure sex appeal. Dangerous Gentry.

Her body was shaking bad from adrenaline, nerves, or maybe both. Gentry didn't seem to mind, though. He only smiled wider in the moment before his lips pressed against hers.

It was gun-powder meets flame. It wasn't a gentle kiss, or a questioning one. This was hard and focused. He sipped at her lips so hard his teeth scraped her, lifting another wave of chills over her body. His body pressed her against the wall, trapping her, but she felt nothing but safe. She wanted this, wanted him so badly. Not just fooling around this time either, she wanted all of him.

Blaire was ready.

With trembling fingers, she pulled at his belt. God, she was bad at this. It had been too long since she'd asked for this from a man.

He allowed it, even let off a soft, sexy noise deep in his throat when her fingertip brushed the head of his cock. His abs were rigid as she unfastened his pants and shoved them down his thighs. Was that a smile against her lips? Was he laughing at how clumsy she was?

Gentry rolled his hips against her so hard she could feel his erection through the thin material of her leggings. Nope. He wasn't laughing. Maybe he was just happy she was telling him what she wanted? What if she wasn't any good at this? *Stop thinking.*

Gentry cupped her neck with one hand and

dragged her waist hard to him with the other. His kisses deepened, his tongue stroking into her mouth rhythmically. He ran his hands up her ribs, dragging her sweater with them, then pulled it over her head and threw it to the ground. And then he was back on her, kissing her as he unsnapped the back of her bra. At least one of them knew what they were doing. He made quick work of her boots and leggings next, peeling them neatly from her body, panties included. She'd worn black, see-through lace just on the off-chance boning would happen, but Gentry didn't give a fig about her carefully chosen lingerie. Into the pile everything went.

He took off her shirt, so that was the signal, right? He was okay with getting naked? *Seriously, stop thinking!*

With a little growl of frustration with herself, Blaire shoved his sweater up his torso. She wasn't as smooth, but she made up for that in sheer desperation. Sweater removed, she tossed the fabric and then lost her mind. With a squeak, she jumped up like a little flying squirrel aiming for a tree.

Faster than she'd imagined he could, Gentry caught her and wrapped her legs around his hips before he slammed her against the wall and kissed her breathless. He ground his hips, hitting her in just the right spot. God, he was right there, and it felt so good already.

His body was shaking now, too, and that low noise he made was back in his throat. When he spun her away from the wall and settled her on the floor in a rush, her stomach dipped like she was on a roller coaster. Geez, he was strong, and fast.

He grabbed her wrists in one hand and pushed them over her head as he trailed kisses down her throat. Teeth, teeth, Gentry liked scraping her with his teeth. Sexy, bitey man.

The full moon outside was casting everything in blue light, and when Gentry lifted off her and locked his arms against the floor, she got this incredible view of his body. Deep shadows adorned the ridges of his muscles, and the moonlight made his eyes look so bright and striking. Chest heaving, he dragged his hungry gaze from her eyes to her lips to her throat. His attention lingered on her breasts, and she could feel him right at her entrance, the swollen head of his cock dipping shallowly inside her.

"Fff," she murmured, arching her back against

the floor.

"Say it," he growled. "Say something bad, just for me." He trapped her in that blazing green gaze as he pushed into her by inches, stretching her.

"Fuck," she whispered helplessly.

His body rattled with that sexy noise, and she wanted to feel the vibration against her breasts so, enticing him, she rolled her hips to meet his next stroke inside her.

Dominant lover wanted to keep her submissive, though. He wouldn't release her wrists over her head. Instead, he got a smirk that she fell in freaking love with. Naughty man, the devil was in his smile, and she liked it. Liked the tease. Liked being at his mercy.

"Gentry?" she whimpered as he dipped into her shallowly again.

"What do you want, Trouble?"

"You. All of you. Everything. *Please*."

Gentry rolled his hips hard, thrust so deeply into her she cried out with pleasure. Perfect. So perfect, and now he was sliding in and out of her hard and fast. He released her wrists and pulled one of her hands behind his head. Lowering down, he pressed her against the cold wooden floors with his body. Hot and cold. Heat on her front, cool on her back, fire in her middle.

"Gentry!" she cried out as he hit her clit over and over, filling her with a tingling sensation she hadn't felt in so long. Had sex ever felt like this? Like desperation to go farther, go faster, go deeper with a man.

Something was happening. Something big that started in her chest and emanated outward. Her entire body felt like it was glowing from the inside out, and with every pump of his cock inside her, the sensation pulsed stronger.

He spread her legs wider and bucked into her deeper, and she was there. Too soon maybe, but she couldn't stop what was happening. Blaire cried out and gripped the back of his hair hard, raking her nails against his scalp.

The rattle in his throat turned into a feral snarl that should've scared her. It should've terrified her, but Gentry had hit his stride, and orgasm ripped through her in that instant. Gentry buried his face against her neck and bit her, almost too hard, as he rammed forward again. Pulsing ecstasy rippled through her body in the moment he shot warmth into her. He reared back and bucked again with a grunt. His teeth felt so sharp. Pleasure and pain, and then flooding heat as he emptied himself inside her.

"Ow," she squeaked as he worked his jaw, and Gentry's reaction was instant. He released her and pushed up on locked arms.

"Fuck, I'm sorry." His dick was still throbbing inside of her, matching her aftershocks, but there was horror in his eyes as he watched where she was covering her neck with her hand. "Let me see," he said in a voice she almost didn't recognize. It was too low and growly.

His eyes looked like two churning green flames as she pulled her hand away from her neck. He rolled his eyes closed and let off the most relieved sigh she'd ever heard. His body went limp as he rested his forehead against hers and hugged her tightly. "I'm sorry. That was too close. I'm sorry."

"Too close?" she asked, baffled. They'd had sex. The deed was done. They couldn't get much closer than they were right now, connected at the hips, him buried deep inside of her. Plus, she didn't know how it was for him, but to her, it felt like their souls had met.

Gentry rolled to the side, bringing her with him, and hugged her tightly against his chest. He was quiet, but he seemed to need that right now. So she cuddled close to him, immersing herself in his abundant warmth, and waited.

"I've never done this with someone like you," he murmured, his chin resting on the top of her hair. "It was reckless."

It stung like a slap on cold skin. "You've said that before." She was trying to keep the hurt from her voice and failing. "That was good for me. I don't have a ton of experience, Gentry, but for me, that was good. It was special. I don't jump into bed easily, so don't hurt me. Or if you plan on it, let me have tonight. I don't want to feel guilty until tomorrow."

"That's not what I mean. Blaire, you were amazing. That wasn't just some casual fuck for me either. I wish I could tell you..."

And there it was again—the shut-down.

"Tell me what?" she whispered against his chest.

His heart was beating too fast against her cheek. He swallowed audibly. "Everything."

"Why can't you?"

"Because we're different, Blaire. We aren't the

same, no matter how much I wish we were. There are rules."

"What rules?" she asked, completely frustrated.

"Rules against us. Against this."

"Against us hugging?"

"No, against us being together at all. Fuck!" Gentry released her and sat up, ran his hands through his hair and gripped the back of his neck. "The rules are there for a reason, Blaire."

"What reason?"

"To protect me!" He gestured to her neck and looked sick in the blue moonlight. "To protect you."

Blaire sat up and covered her chest. It was cold in here now that Gentry had stolen his warmth away. And if she was honest, she felt a whole lot more vulnerable right now. She shouldn't because she'd wanted this. She'd craved intimacy with him, and they'd connected on a level she'd never experienced. But she didn't understand what was happening with Gentry, and she didn't get the dynamics at play. "Is this you letting me go early?" she murmured.

"No." He gritted his teeth so hard a muscle in his jaw jumped. He opened his mouth to say more, but froze. All but his eyes, which flicked to the window behind her.

The expression on his face said there was something there, watching through the cracked window.

"What is it?" she asked, too terrified to turn around.

"Get dressed," Gentry said low.

"Oh, my gosh," she huffed out as she bolted for the wall where her clothes lay in a pile. She wasn't even into her sweater when a long, low howl lifted into the air.

Gentry wasn't sitting anymore, but was instead leaned against the window sill on locked arms, glaring outside. He shoved off, shaking his head, and it was then that she could hear it. There was a rattling in his throat, but it was different than before. It was scary, and the moon was playing tricks on his eye color again. Something was happening with Gentry that she didn't understand.

He stalked to the door as another howl lifted on the air to join the first. "Stay here. Lock the door."

"You're going to go out there with those wolves? That's a terrible idea! We should call the police!"

"No police. That'll make this so much worse. I'll

be back. Don't let anyone in. No one but me." His gaze lingered on her a moment more, and then he murmured, "Please trust me." Gentry disappeared into the night, closing the door firmly behind him.

Trust me.

He'd just given her a half-answer on everything she'd asked, and he wanted her to trust him?

He'd just walked out into the snowy night...naked! With the wolves. Not just one anymore, but two!

With shaking hands, she dressed, shoved her feet into her snow boots, didn't bother lacing them up, then bolted for the phone.

She dialed 911, but hesitated to connect the call. She just stood there, staring at the glowing screen of her cell phone. Why did this feel like jumping off a cliff and into a river she didn't know the depths of? She could sink down and bob back up for air or slam into the shallow, rocky bottom. Doing this after he'd asked her not to felt like a betrayal, but she wanted him to be okay.

"Shoot," she said on a terrified breath. Blaire bolted for the window, but Gentry was gone, and the howling came to a sudden stop. The song just disappeared like it had never been there at all.

Wolves, this place trashed, the mysteries that surrounded Gentry's father, Gentry's eyes, baffling answers, and *someone like you, someone like you, someone like you.*

Her head spun as she searched the night woods outside desperately for any sign of the man she was getting closer to and farther away from all at once.

Please trust me. His voice seemed to plead on the crisp wind.

Blaire deleted the emergency number and set her phone on the window sill. Calling the police would push Gentry away, and then she would never get answers. She would always wonder what if? What if she'd listened, what if she'd trusted him, what if she'd stayed in this and backed his play?

He hadn't seemed scared, only angry, and he'd gone out into the night with an air of confidence. Was he crazy? Nah. Some bone-deep instinct told her that wasn't it.

Instead, Gentry was dealing with demons she couldn't see yet.

But she wanted to.

ELEVEN

Asher's howl lifted again, calling Gentry's wolf from him. He grunted in pain as he pitched forward onto his hands and knees in the snow. What was happening to him?

Another thirty seconds in Winter's Edge, and he would've Changed right in front of Blaire. Fucking Asher was forcing a Change, but he shouldn't be able to.

Gentry's bones snapped, and he gritted his teeth against the pain. At least he was far enough into the woods that the night shadows hid him from Blaire's view. God, he didn't want to do this.

Roman's howl lifted into the air, but his tone drifted right over Gentry's skin. The second Asher howled again, though, Gentry cried out as the wolf ripped from his body.

Wolf came out pissed and charging the woods. Asher and Roman were calling for war way too close to his mate. They had almost exposed him to her, and way too soon. Wolf wanted Blaire, but he had to be a patient hunter, or she would run. She would get scared and wouldn't understand she belonged to Wolf. He would never hurt her. Only protect her. Even from his own brothers.

He was going to bleed Asher for pulling that shit, and Roman for helping. Logic tried to keep quiet with his dislike for his brothers, but Wolf didn't have those hang-ups. He hated them, therefore he would hurt them.

He sprinted through the fresh snow. He could smell them, scents that would never leave him. He'd grown up with them, would know them anywhere. Did they even remember him? Had they even cared when they left? Had they even thought about how destroyed he'd been when they'd turned their disdain on him and cut him off? Cut him out? Fuck them both.

Asher came charging out of the shadows, a beast of a wolf, thick-furred and black as tar. He was bigger than Gentry remembered, but it had been a long-ass time since he'd seen his brothers. Gentry was bigger now, too, and trained for this kind of brawl.

Neither of them slowed. They just clashed like two storms. Asher was a ripper now, a reaper, a titan fueled by bad blood, but Gentry had fury on his side. The fear in Blaire's eyes flashed through his mind as he sank his teeth into Asher's shoulder and jerked his powerful neck. When warmth sprayed across his face, he grew drunk with satisfaction. Bloodlust did that. Hatred did that.

Pain blasted through his backend when Roman joined the battle. The baby of the family wasn't a baby anymore. He wasn't some lanky pup. He was a monster, the same size as Gentry with gold eyes. His wolf was like the werewolves of legend. Blood-splattered teeth, hate in his glowing eyes, muzzle snarled up, the promise of death written all over his face. Good. Wolf wouldn't have to mourn when he killed him.

He spun and lunged at Roman's front paw, caught it in a blur, and snapped the bone with a hard bite. The yelp of pain echoed through the clearing, and with the sound came a tornado. That's all Wolf could think to describe it. The snow around them shot straight up into the sky, creating a wall of white, and thick, black power pulsed against Wolf's skin. It made him sick to his stomach.

Beside him, Asher and Roman froze, their attention on the dark shadow that was walking slowly through the wall of snow, hands out.

It was the woman from the store, the dark-haired one in the old truck. The familiar one. With every step of her approach, the sick feeling in Gentry's gut grew until his legs buckled under him. His body was on fire, and it wasn't just him. Asher and Roman were in the snow, writhing.

"Change back!" the woman screamed, her voice crackling with the power of the wind, but her lips hadn't moved.

Agony ripped through Gentry, and he closed his eyes against the black magic forcing his Change into his human skin. Back to Logic.

Teeth bared, Asher was dragging his breaking body toward her by his front paws.

"Uh uuuh," she sang softly, shaking her head as she took a step back.

Asher, Asher, Asher. Change back. The whispered

words hadn't come from her lips, but were bouncing around in Gentry's head.

The last of the Change blasted through Gentry's body, and he winced away from the view of Asher breaking slowly, bones snapping one at a time like dry twigs, and blood pooling in the snow beneath his body.

"Give in," Roman yelled, completely human. "Asher!"

Asher imploded into his human self, and the snow wall fell to the ground around them.

Every cell in Gentry's body was on fire, and he retched in the snow. He clenched his fists before he slammed them to the ground and tried to breathe through the agony. "Who are you?" Gentry choked out.

"Can't you feel it?" Roman asked from beside him. He was on his hands and knees, arm wrapped around his stomach, body trembling, eyes bright gold like his wolf wasn't sleeping yet. He wore a full beard now and looked like a fucking bodybuilder. Roman was almost unrecognizable compared to the boy Gentry had known. "She's a witch."

"You're welcome," the woman barked out, eyes

flashing with anger.

"For what?" Asher growled out.

"Look at you! Brothers, bleeding each other like animals."

"We are animals."

"Bullshit! That's bullshit. Your father would be ashamed if he saw what you'd just done. You were going to kill each other!"

Asher tossed Roman a frown, but didn't even bother to look at Gentry. "You knew our father?"

Pain washed across the woman's face, and she stared off into the woods for a few moments before she answered. "I loved your father." Her lip trembled, and her eyebrows lifted. "We weren't allowed, for obvious reasons, but he was mine, and I was his. Losing him was the worst day of my life. But seeing you three, looking so much like him, going to war out here is a close second."

"My wolf looks nothing like that asshole," Asher ground out, his chin tucked to his chest as he glared up at the woman from his knees.

"Not your wolf, Asher Striker. Your eyes. You have his fire. He was always scared for you because of it. And you," she said, arcing her gaze to Roman.

"You have his build. Height, arms, hands, all the same. And it doesn't matter how thick you grow that beard, boy. You can't hide his face. He marked you up better than the rest. But you," she murmured, blinking slowly and giving her attention to Gentry. "You're the one he passed his wolf to. Can you feel him separately I wonder? Hmm, Gentry? Does he feel like a different creature living inside of your body? Your father struggled with the same, and your wolf is the spitting image of his. Get up, monsters."

Gentry waited for the tendrils of black magic to curdle his stomach again, but she wasn't using her power anymore. And when he studied her closer, the woman was swaying slightly on her feet. A quick glance at Asher, who was closest to her, and he had his narrowed eyes on her shaking hands.

A witch she may be, but all-powerful she was not. She'd drained herself. They could kill her now with a single bite. She wasn't a wolf, probably wouldn't survive it, but Gentry had a hundred questions rattling around in his mind, so he played along and stood slowly. Every muscle in his body was twitching like he'd been electrocuted, but he splayed his legs and kept his balance.

"What's your name?" he gritted out.

"Odine."

"Odine what?" Roman asked.

She inhaled deeply and lifted her chin proudly. "Odine Striker. Get your shit together long enough to spread your father's ashes in the wind. His soul is at unrest. He wanted his sons to do it, and you've put it off too long." Odine turned and strode off, her snow boots crunching as she stepped over the piles of snow she'd raised like a tidal wave and dropped back down to earth like an avalanche. "I want to be there. I deserve to be there."

Roman tossed Gentry a what-the-hell look, then asked, "Okay, how do we find you?"

Odine disappeared into the shadows like a ghost, but her voice bounced around the woods. "You don't. I'll find you when you're ready."

Gentry shook his head hard to rid himself of her words, still rattling around in his skull.

"A witch," Roman ground out. "Dad was fucking a witch."

"Not just fucking," Asher murmured, running his hand over the short crop of dirty blond hair, the same shade as Gentry and Roman's. "Dad gave her his last name. A human witch." He slid a suspicious glare to Gentry. "Did you know, Favorite?"

"Don't you fucking call me that, asshole. Obviously, I wasn't a favorite. I don't know any of the shit that went down. Dad kept everything from me."

"He gave you the fucking inn and bar, man," Roman said. "Asher and I got jack squat. So fucking predictable. We always got jack squat! He didn't even leave us a damn hunting rifle to remember him by." Roman put a stick in his mouth and bit down, then hunched into himself and set his broken wrist.

The crunch of the bone made Gentry wince. He'd done that. No, Wolf had. The separate entity Odine had guessed at.

Crimson was dripping down from Asher's shoulder to his fingertips. *Drip, drop, drip, drop,* more red snow. His neck was chewed up, too, just like Gentry's. They were all shredded and bloody and, yeah, if Odine hadn't come, there would have been bodies tonight.

He didn't even want to guess how a witch knew they were out here at war with each other. Probably had a damn crystal ball or something.

A friggin' witch. He'd known they existed, just

never met one. Never wanted to.

"Gentry?" Blaire asked from behind him.

Startled, he spun. She shouldn't have been able to sneak up on him like that. She stood leaning heavily against a tree, her hand to her stomach. Red was streaming between her fingertips, and agony was etched into every beautiful line of her face.

"Blaire?"

"Whose Blaire?" Roman asked, as Gentry bolted for her.

She pitched forward, coughing blood, but he knelt in time to catch her. Only when she hit his hands, she turned to ashes.

"Blaire?" he yelled, horrified.

"There's no one there, psychopath," Roman called.

"Does anyone else see the wolves?" Asher asked in a disturbed voice.

"Like the new pack?" Roman asked.

"No. They're all dead. Like…zombie wolves. They're missing their skin."

Gentry stood in a rush and shook imaginary ashes off his hands. He had to check on Blaire. There were no zombie wolves, but he knew what this was.

This was remnants of that damn black magic Odine had used. Nothing good would come from these woods until it had dissipated. Heart hammering against his sternum, he climbed over the steep bank of snow and sprinted toward Winter's Edge.

"Where are you going?" Roman called.

Gentry didn't want them anywhere near Blaire, though, so he ignored the question and ducked a low-hanging tree branch. They wouldn't understand.

But some deep-rooted instinct said something was very, very wrong here.

TWELVE

Blaire paced in front of the window. Minutes ago, the earth had shaken, and the echo of wolves snarling had been so loud it had filled Winter's Edge. And then the sounds had been drowned out by a massive whoosh. White snow powder had blasted up into the sky like an unending explosion. Her stomach felt queasy, from nerves, yes, but from something darker, too. Something just above her senses.

A back door blasted open and slammed against the wall, and when Blaire spun around, a man she'd never seen before stalked out of the kitchen. His face was canted, and his eyes were a strange silver color. He had short hair and tattoos down the right side of his body. He was tall and built like a brick house, but every step he stalked closer was completely silent. Not a single board under his feet dared to utter a squeak. He was completely naked, but didn't move to cover himself, and he chugged breath like he'd run a great distance to get here. Subdued power hummed through his body. Something about him reminded her of Gentry. Behind him, another man came out of the kitchen and jumped up on the bar top like the height was nothing at all. His eyes were like liquid gold, and he lifted his head higher into the air, nostrils flaring slightly. Both of them had rivers of blood streaming down their bodies.

She'd never seen two more terrifying men in all her life.

A whimper clawed its way up her throat, but she couldn't turn and run no matter how much she wanted to. Instinct told her not to give these predators her back. The flickering lantern light made them look like monsters.

"Take another step closer to her, and I'll kill you," Gentry said blandly from where he stood in the doorway. His voice threatened violence, and for a moment, she thought he would kill them. He stood stone-like against the blue moonlight, every muscle in his body rigid as he chugged frozen breath. His eyes were reflecting oddly, like an animal's, and a sudden trill of fear zinged up her spine.

Gentry wasn't human.

She dragged her gaze to the others, both staring at her with matching hungry expressions.

They didn't just look like monsters.

They *were* monsters.

"Blaire?" the tall silver-eyed one asked in a snarling voice.

Blood was dripping from his hand to the floor in a puddle, but he didn't favor any of his injuries, and they were many.

"H-how do you know my name?"

The man snarled up his lips over bright white teeth and gave Gentry a hate-filled glare. "You know what she is. That's not a question, Favorite. I know you can fuckin' smell her."

"Yeah, she also smells like sex, and you," the bearded man crouched on the bar top said to Gentry. "Are you fucking humans—"

"Roman, stop!" the tall one barked out, cutting him off.

Humans. He'd been about to ask Gentry if he was

fucking humans now. Blaire backed toward the wall slowly.

Movements slow and calculated, Gentry maneuvered himself gracefully between Blaire and the others, his back to her, and now she could hear it clearly—that snarl in his throat. She'd thought it was habit, and he'd been quiet about it, but now it sounded like an animal. It sounded like a wolf.

Tears blurred her vision as her back hit the wall. She'd never been more terrified in her life.

"Blaire, no one will hurt you." Gentry tossed her a glance over his shoulder. "You have to settle down or you'll set them off."

"No one will hurt her?" Roman asked, jumping off the counter and barely making a sound as he landed. "What you're doing is punishable by death, Gentry. Yours and hers."

"Roman," the other man warned.

"Fuck off, Asher." Roman cast him a glare and dragged his attention back to Blaire before Gentry cut off her line of sight with his wide shoulders. "No wonder you were a favorite, Gentry. No wonder! Dad saw you in him, right? Human fucker? He was doing it and saw the same weakness in his favorite boy. Made him love you even more. Made me and Asher invisible because we weren't weak like you!" Roman yelled the last three words, and Blaire jumped hard. "This will get you killed. It'll get her killed. It'll get me and Asher killed. This ain't your town anymore! It's Rhett's, and he *will* use this as an excuse to end the Striker line. And why the fuck is Winter's Edge trashed?"

"I don't know, Roman! Back the fuck off!"

"You were supposed to be running this place, right? Destiny and all. Instead, Dad died alone, unprotected, and his legacy is trashed, and what are you doing?" Roman jammed a finger at Blaire and raised his eyebrows at Gentry.

One last step was all Gentry allowed before he blurred to the man and blasted him across the face. But Roman was ready and hooked his arm around the back of Gentry's neck, taking them both to the ground. And there they went to work pummeling each other.

"Gentry!" Blaire screamed as he slammed the man against the hardwood floor.

Asher was searching the thrashed liquor cabinet like there wasn't this awful frenzied fight happening in the middle of the bar.

"Do something!" she pleaded with Asher as Gentry lifted Roman into the air and slammed him onto a table, shattering it to splinters.

Asher tossed her a slit-eyed glare as though offended she'd even talk to him and went back to searching cabinets. He found a bottle of what looked like Jim Beam and took a long drag, tossed the cap onto the counter, and then walked out the way he came without a second glance for the two clashing titans.

Fury blasted through her. Enough was enough, and everyone had bled all over the brand new clean floors. She'd been lied to, and she was pissed! Adrenaline pumping through her, she screeched at Roman, who was straddling Gentry, pounding his face. Dicks everywhere. Dicks and blood and bruises and scars and tattoos, and these men were freaking ridiculous. Blaire picked up a ladder back chair, and before she could stop herself, she swung it like a bat and shattered the old wooden seat across Roman's back.

The bearded man rocked forward and froze, his fist clenched mid-air. Gentry had his hand on

Roman's throat, and his face was beat red, but when Roman turned a slow, deadly golden gaze on her, she instantly regretted getting involved.

"Accident?" she tried with her face scrunched up.

"Are you trying to die faster?" Roman gritted out.

Blaire stomped her snow boot on the floor. "That's enough! I didn't ask for any of this…this…whatever is happening! I've been through hell, and I'm having a nice break from work, and I like Gentry the whatever-he-is. He's cute and a little terrifying, but mostly nice, and there will be no more death-talk on my fucking vacation."

"You said fucking," Gentry muttered from the floor. His lip was split, but he was smiling.

Roman shoved off him, stood, circled back, and kicked him in the ribs, but Gentry just blocked him and said, "You kick like a girl."

Roman flipped him off and then flipped Blaire off, too, before he strode out the door, still butt-naked. He tried to slam the door behind him, but it gently swung closed, and he roared a sound of pure frustration.

Gentry stood slowly and rested one hand on his hip. He pressed the back of his wrist onto his bloody lip as he glared out the window at Roman, who was stomping through the snow like an angry yeti.

At a complete loss on how to tackle anything that had just happened, Blaire murmured, "Well, tonight was weird."

Chest heaving, body shredded, naked as a jaybird and shaking, Gentry gave her a strange look, trapping her in that wild green gaze of his for a few moments. Suddenly, he let off a single laugh.

"I have a hundred questions," she admitted.

"Well, I can't answer any of them, so swallow those back down."

"Fantastic. Can I ask you one question I think you *can* answer?" She had a hunch, but she wanted to know for sure.

"Fine," Gentry muttered, shifting his weight.

"Whoooo are those terrifying men?"

Gentry rolled his eyes closed and sighed. When he looked at her again, his expression was exhausted. "Those would be my brothers."

THIRTEEN

Well, last night had been terrific. Blaire poked the dark circles under her eyes. Her dreams had been riddled with avalanches and monsters chasing her through the woods, and she'd given up on sleep sometime around five this morning.

Vacations were supposed to be sleeping in and rest and relaxation, but the Striker brothers had taken all sense of safety away from her. Well, except Gentry. As much as she tried to convince herself he was scary, he'd been tender with her last night, and then put himself in front of her and protected her from Roman.

What she needed was a day away from this place for some clarity, so she could wrap her head around what was actually going on in Rangeley. This wasn't some fun mystery to unravel anymore. There was an entire supernatural dynamic here that she knew nothing about. And from the mention of the rules and the deadly consequences, she was pretty sure she would never find out.

And now her head and heart were all mixed up. Head said Gentry was dangerous to get involved with, but heart didn't care. Heart thought this was a great idea, to attach to a man of a different...species? Was this even okay? He wasn't human, and she was, and maybe there were rules because it was wrong. Or something. Also, in addition to her head and heart was her needy vagina that kept her eyes on the prize, and that was another tempting body-smush with Sexy Gentry. Couldn't be wrong, not if it had felt this right.

She glared at her tired face in the mirror and applied an extra layer of concealer to cover the dark circles. Then she plumped her lips with a glossy pink and pulled her jacket and purse off the chair in the bedroom.

Blaire let the door bang closed behind her and jogged down the porch stairs with a bounce in her step.

"Mornin', human." Roman called from the porch of the smallest cabin next door. He was clad in teal underwear, a faux-fur winter hat with ear flaps, and unlaced snow boots. He was also eating a bowl of cereal.

"Question," she said, coming to a stop in front of the porch and doing her best not to look at his big dick bulging in his undies. "When would you say it's too early for day drinking?"

Roman slurped a bite of cereal, and with a full mouth said, "No such thing as too early."

"That was my first instinct, too." She turned, but hesitated. "Aren't you cold?"

"I don't get cold."

"Terrific. Stay weird, Roman."

"Will do. Hey human?" Roman called.

"Yeees," she drawled, annoyed with the nickname. She knew what he was doing. He was making sure she knew she was separate from the rest of them. "Gentry left you a present in the front seat of your car. I opened it." His eyes weren't gold anymore, but a vivid sky blue as they narrowed. "You're playing a dangerous game. Both of you are. One that will get you hurt."

"Is that a threat?"

Roman gave her an empty smile. "A promise."

Something moved behind him, and Blaire startled hard when Asher stood from a rocking chair and approached the railing. He locked his arms against it and dragged his gaze down her body and back to her face. She hadn't even realized he was there, he'd been so still.

"Blaire Hayward, acquisitions editor for Always Ink Publisher, divorced, and human. Bad match in more ways than one." He jerked his chin toward the big cabin, ten-ten, where Gentry stayed. "I have no spare love for my brother, but he deserves better than a mate who doesn't know how to stick around and will get him killed."

Asher's words shocked her into a moment of slack-jawed silence.

"One, I'm human, and clearly you aren't. Great. I have no idea what all that entails, but Gentry doesn't feel so different from me, so stop being such a prejudiced...Asherhole!"

Roman snorted and repeated, "Asherhole."

"Furthermore, that sticking around comment?

It's none of your business, but the divorce wasn't my choice! I didn't file the papers. What did you want me to do? Never sign them and cling to a man who didn't want me? Don't make judgements on things you know nothing about. I was destroyed, and I'm just now finding my way back to myself, and yeah, Gentry has my attention. He makes me feel like…like…*me* again!" Disproportionately angry, she lost her mind and chucked her car keys at Asher's face.

Annoyingly, he plucked them out of the air before they hit him, and Blaire regretted her actions. She wished she could stomp to the car and speed away, spraying them both with snow from her tires, but… "I need those back," she muttered, holding her pink mitten-clad hand up to him. Impatiently, she wiggled her fingers.

Roman was wearing a big, dumb grin as he looked back and forth from Blaire to Asher and back again.

She could've sworn she saw the faintest smirk on Asher's face as he leaned over the railing and settled the keys onto her palm. "I wouldn't drink at the tavern if I were you."

"I wouldn't tell me what to do… if I were *you*!

So..." She was angry and terrible with comebacks, so she tried to flip him off, but her finger only bulged against her pink mitten. Roman laughed harder, and there was a smile on Asher's face.

Stupid Strikers. They made her want to be unladylike and rude.

Blaire kicked a snow drift away from the door of her car and got in. Sure enough, there was an unwrapped gift on her passenger's seat. It was a paperback copy of a werewolf erotica book called *Bang Me, Fang Me*. Her anger evaporated, and Blaire snorted as she studied the cover.

Inside the front flap, there was a handwritten note that was already unfolded and likely read by Nosey Roman.

Trouble,

I can't answer questions, but I can give you this, another belated birthday present. Everything in it is wrong, but entertaining. I checked the sex scenes and I'm sorry to tell you, but there was no sign of baby gravy. I hope you enjoy the read anyway. Relax. This isn't for work. Just for fun. I'll give you the space you need. Call me if you want.

Chaos

His phone number was scribbled at the bottom.

"Are you mushy smiling?" Roman asked from where he was staring into her window with his hands cupped around his face. "I get why he calls you Trouble, but why do you call him Chaos? And what's baby gravy? Is that some human flirting thing? I've never seen this before. It's gross, but it's like one of those medical shows where you are repulsed, but at the same time you can't look away."

Blaire sighed tiredly and started her car. "Have a good day, Roman," she gritted out through clenched teeth.

"You broke a chair over my back, Blaire. You owe me answers—"

"I said good day!" She hit the gas and felt a little guilty that part of her wished she would accidently run over Roman's foot.

She searched Gentry's house longingly, but he wasn't there, and his truck wasn't parked out front anymore either. Okay, that was a good thing. Now she wouldn't be tempted to turn around and jump back in with him too quickly. Time to herself was essential today. Her hormones would make her forget all the craziness that happened last night, and she would jump his bones when she should really be taking serious consideration whether to stay here any longer.

Oh, she believed Asher and Roman when they talked about how much trouble they were in. Those two men had scared the ever-lovin' poop out of her last night, and they were allies. Kind of. Well, at least they were family to Gentry. Also kind of because she didn't understand why they all seemed to hate each other so much. And right about now she was thanking all her lucky stars she was an only child because, apparently, the Strikers healed faster than the average human, but they were still black-and-blue today from wailing on each other.

Last night, snow had fountained into the air, high above the trees, like an upside-down waterfall. Could werewolves do that? She would've loved to ask a million questions, but she had tried last night with Gentry, and though he'd looked sick about it the entire walk from Winter's Edge to her cabin, he'd denied her answers.

"It's safer for you if you don't know," he'd explained.

So, this was the type of relationship she could look forward to until she went home. A surface relationship where they both pretended they were the same kind of mammal and avoided all conversations about anything serious or important. Sex with Gentry had been mind-blowing, beautiful, and so satisfying, but a big part of her wanted more with him than just a physical connection. She wanted him to trust her, and she really wanted to trust him, too.

It was stormy out and snowing once again. Thick flurries drifted down, piling onto her windshield, so she turned on the wipers and squinted up at the churning gray clouds. She wouldn't see sunshine today.

She glanced at the book cover again and shook her head. Werewolves existed. So much made sense now. The way he'd seemed so serious when he'd asked if she read paranormal romance. How he'd asked her to trust him and not call the cops. How he'd dragged that dead turkey off her porch. He'd canceled breakfast due to no sleep. Was that because he'd been the wolf that night?

Someone like you. How many times had she heard that since she'd come to Rangeley? And not just from Gentry, but from the man she'd asked directions from that first day. Perhaps he was a werewolf, too. Maybe everyone in this town was but her.

That was an unsettling thought.

Blaire coasted around a bend, but when she saw the massive gray wolf sitting in the middle of the snowy road, she gasped and locked up the brakes. The car skidded sideways on the slick straightaway, but came to a rocking stop before she slid into the animal.

Green eyes. That was the first thing she noticed. They were bright and the exact shade Gentry's had been last night. He was huge, much bigger than she imagined wild wolves to be. Even sitting, he was as tall as the top of her window. He had a big barrel chest, and his fur was dark gray with a touch of lighter gray mottled throughout. He had darker points and a black nose. His paws were huge, splayed against the snow and ice.

He was just watching her, but without warning, he tossed his head back and let off a long, haunting note. His breath froze in the air and looked like smoke rising above him.

It. Was. Beautiful. The sound and Gentry both.

She moved to open the door, but Gentry lowered

his head and let the howl die in his throat, eyes flashing with warning. And then he stood, much taller than she'd realized, and padded gracefully to the trees that lined the road. He paused on the edge, his eyes looking bright surrounded by that storm-gray fur. His back was to her, but he stared at her over his shoulder.

She didn't want to leave. This moment was profound. He'd let her see him, let her in. And everything in her screamed he wasn't allowed to do this. Not with her. Not with a human. He was taking a huge risk because he cared deeply. About her. *He cared.*

She wanted to cry and laugh and cry some more with the realization because she was in this, too. She felt the same. If the roles were reversed, she would take risks to show him he mattered.

Gentry trotted into the woods with such an unnaturally smooth gait, she couldn't take her gaze from him until he disappeared into the brush. He'd looked so powerful, so rugged, so dangerous, and so beautiful all at once. If she wasn't staring right at the distinct wolf prints in the snow near her window, she would've tried to convince herself it hadn't happened.

How could it? Science said two species couldn't occupy the same body. But maybe Gentry and his brothers were formed from magic instead, something she'd never believed in.

Her world had just been flipped upside down.

Blaire eased onto the gas and straightened out the car. She'd had these grand plans today to convince herself the supernatural hadn't taken over this town. She was supposed to go out and meet people to convince herself all was normal around here. She'd planned on convincing herself that last night had happened differently than it did, but Gentry had taken all the uncertainty away from her, as if he had known she needed physical proof of what he was. Of what dwelled inside of him.

Gentry was a werewolf, and there was no more questioning back and forth. There was no more black and white anymore. Gentry and his brothers were the gray area that didn't make scientific sense in this world, but that existed anyway.

She, Blaire Annalee Hayward, had fallen in love with a werewolf.

This wasn't the destiny she'd imagined for herself. She was vanilla. Matt had called her "too bland" when he'd given her the divorce papers. He'd said she bored him, and that his life was so un-exciting, he couldn't pretend to love her another day.

That had been her life, though. Boring but safe, and now look what had happened? Fate had just laughed. Fate had spun her 180 degrees in a tornado wind and was watching her try to find her way through unfamiliar territory.

But so what? Blaire grinned as she took a right at the rundown Hunter Cove Inn sign. Maybe her life was meant to have an adventure like this. Maybe her life had been bland before to prepare her for a man like Gentry, so she could appreciate him more. A relationship with him would never, ever be dull.

The radio was on low, but a song came on about belonging down below. It had a heavy drum beat, and the base was hitting hard. Blaire turned up the radio dial and laughed at the lyrics. The song was talking about a good girl gone bad. Well-played Fate.

She drove into town blaring it and sang with the chorus the second time around at the top of her lungs.

Eff you, Matt. No...fuck you, Matt. Yeah, that felt better.

Gentry had never once made her feel boring or like the color beige. He'd empowered her and been amused when she was sassy. That man had the devil in him in the form of a wolf, and maybe that was okay because, right now, Blaire felt like a dragon was growing inside of her, too.

She pulled in front of a coffee shop with a big front porch. On the porch were four rocking chairs situated around a wood burning stove that was steaming with heat. Sweet! She could read her dirty werewolf book and drink hot chocolate and actually vacation! No work.

She wished Gentry was here, so she could cuddle up in a blanket in the chair, slip her feet under his butt to keep them warm, and then sneak peeks at him whenever she wanted. Which was all the time. Something about that man held her attention.

The barista was nice to her in the coffee shop. She was probably human. Blaire was assuming the werewolves in this town were rude and hated strangers, so the nice people she met today would probably be humans like her.

Blaire collected her giant hot chocolate and dusted off the rocking chair closest to the flames, then sat down and opened her book to chapter one, clutching the hot cup to her chest to warm herself.

She had blasted through Chapter Four before she realized someone was sitting next to her. She was at a dirty part, so her cheeks flushed at being busted.

The woman grinned knowingly and gestured to Blaire's book. "Do you read sex books in public often?"

"No, but I want to," Blaire said cheekily.

"You know Gentry Striker?" the woman asked.

The smile fell from Blaire's face so fast she felt her ears move. Werewolf? "Who wants to know?"

"It sounds like you just asked me if I was friend or foe," the black-haired woman said, warming her hands by the fire.

"And?"

She slid Blaire a glance with her twinkling, black eyes. "Friend." The woman was pretty, with a straight nose and smile lines on her face. She was in her early sixties perhaps, and silver streaked back from her temples in a striking way. "I've seen you before."

"In town?"

"Nope." She pointed to her temple. "In here. Been waiting on you to get here."

"I don't understand."

"There was a mix-up at the realtor's office, right? Gentry was looking for a long-term renter, but he got you instead."

Blaire sat straight up and settled her book carefully into her lap. "That was your doing?"

She dipped her chin once.

"Why?"

"Lots of reasons, both for you and him. Mostly because Gentry needs someone to push him to his potential. And I'm guessing you need the same."

It suddenly felt uncomfortably cold under the woman's stare. "I should go." Blaire stood to leave, but the woman said, "You have questions your man can't answer." She arched one delicate eyebrow. "I can."

Blaire looked longingly at her car. She didn't like how much this woman knew, but it was also seriously tempting to get some answers that she may never get from Gentry. Slowly, she sat back down and scanned the street. No one seemed to be paying attention to them.

"What kind of answers."

"First, let me introduce myself." The woman

offered her hand. “I’m Odine.”

Pretty name. “I’m Blaire, but I have a feeling you already knew that,” she said, shaking the woman’s warm hand.

Odine smiled her answer, then flipped Blaire’s hand over and looked at her palm. She traced the big line that curved around her thumb. “Broken life line.” Her voice was thoughtful. Troubled perhaps.

“I don’t believe in that stuff,” Blaire murmured, pulling her hand away.

“Hmm,” Odine said, her eyes tightening in the corners. “Perhaps someday you will. You’ve only recently learned that monsters exist, yes?”

Blaire swallowed hard. “Are you a monster?”

“Not the kind you’re thinking of. I’m human, like you. Also like you, I fell for a wolf, which is why I have the answers you will likely never pry from Gentry. This town is a hub for the supernatural. Something about Rangeley attracts them. Maybe it’s the low human population in the winter months, or the miles of woods that surround this place. Maybe it’s the ample game or the rich history of supernaturals in these parts.” Odine gave her a conspiratorial grin and leaned forward, lowering her voice. “Or perhaps it’s the stuff you don't believe in that attracts the nightmares."

"Gentry isn't a nightmare."

"I wasn't speaking of your mate."

"His brothers?"

"To be decided. Roman and Asher are on the fence. Good on one side. Evil on the other. Which way will they jump? I don't know that answer yet, but they won't stay on the fence much longer. Gentry has always been on the right side of the fence. He has his father's moral compass, and it points due north. It causes...tension...between him and his brothers. They are more like their mother, but he is his father's child. It bodes good for you."

"You called him my mate."

"You were his mate before he even laid eyes on you."

Unsure, Blaire laughed. "But...I was married."

"And how did that work out for you?"

Anger blasted through her. "That ended because we were broken, not because I belonged to someone else."

"You always belonged to Gentry," Odine said sharply. "Your ex was preparation for what you will go through in Rangeley."

Blaire shook her head and inhaled deeply. This was crazy. Odine was clearly insane.

"You don't believe in destiny either?" Odine asked innocently. "You will."

Blaire scooted to the edge of her chair to leave, but Odine reached forward in a rush and plucked a few strands of hair from Blaire's head. She turned them over in her hand, where they hovered, caught fire, and turned to ash in an instant. There was a heaviness to the air that clogged Blaire's throat.

Odine's eyes never left hers as she removed her palm from under the floating ashes and let them drop to the snow. "No, I have the right person. You felt a deep connection to him the second you saw him. You wanted him to touch you, body and soul. You knew on a cellular level that he could repair the damage that's been done to you."

"Stop," Blaire pleaded, terrified.

"I'm not telling you this to scare you, child." Odine's eyes softened. "I've been there, right where you are. I've been there with my wolf, and it was scary, it was beautiful, and I wish it had been different for me." Odine pitched her voice louder. "It can be different for you and Gentry. Change is needed in this town. You. Are. That. Change."

Blaire looked around, panicked, because she could feel eyes on her. Three men had stopped on the sidewalk and were watching her with angry, glowing eyes.

"Why are you telling me this here?" she whispered to Odine.

The softness in Odine's eyes left in a flash and was replaced by anger. "Because we're gonna stir up the hive, you and I, Blaire Hayward. Piss off the queen bee who fancies himself a demigod here. He took something precious from me. We'll put pressure on him to react and force Gentry to step up for this town. Force the other Strikers to pick a side and jump the goddamn fence either way."

"You said you were a friend," Blaire said on a horrified breath.

"You won't see it for a while yet," Odine said, leaning back into her rocking chair, "but I am."

She sure as heck didn't feel like any ally Blaire wanted. Furious, she stood and slammed her empty hot chocolate cup into the trash before she jogged down the stairs and past the werewolves glaring her down. The closest one was growling, and fear pushed her legs faster to the driver's side of her rental car.

Blaire had wanted a relaxing day in town, but that woman had just exposed her to a black, pulsing vein of supernatural shit in this town. Worse than that, Odine had exposed Gentry, and that made Blaire angrier than anything.

She backed out of the parking space in a rush and kept checking the rearview mirror on her way down Main Street. The three men with the glowing eyes were gathered in the middle of the road talking and watching her speed toward Hunter Cove.

Odine had told her she had answers, but all she'd done was confuse Blaire more with her riddles. She'd used her for something bad, but for the life of her, Blaire couldn't understand what.

Something told her she'd just been dumped into Rangeley's dark underbelly, and she'd dragged Gentry right down with her.

FOURTEEN

Blaire rolled down her window as she pulled up to where Roman was chopping wood outside the smallest cabin. "Where's Gentry?" she asked him.

"Fuck if I know, I'm not his keeper," Roman said as he put another log on the chopping block.

Irritated, she asked, "Is he still a wolf?"

Roman spun and strode to her window. When he gripped it with his massive hands, Blaire leaned away from him. "You need to stop using terms you don't know anything about, and quick. You two aren't careful—"

"Some woman named Odine just outed me and Gentry in town. Loudly."

"Fuck!" The car door groaned, and when Roman

shoved away from it, there were two indented handprints.

Blaire gave an offended sound and tried to roll up the window, but it just made a bunch of clicking sounds. "Roman! This is a rental!"

"Well, I wouldn't worry about it too much now, Blaire! You won't be returning it in this lifetime. Rhett will have you put down by sunset!" Roman's eyes weren't blue anymore, but were the bright gold from last night. "Three hours. Asher!" he yelled at the cabin before he turned back to laying into her. "Three hours, and you exposed your relationship. That has to be some kind of friggin' record."

"I didn't do it. I was trying to read my book. That lady approached me! And she burned some of my hair and frankly, she was a little scary, so I don't need you yelling at me right now."

"What's happened?" Asher asked as he was jogged down the stairs.

Roman was typing something into his cell phone, but muttered, "Gentry and Princess Human have been outed to the pack. Is witchcraft one word or two? Princess Human got some of her hair burned by Psychodine. Oh, here it is." His lips moved as he read silently, then he nodded. “Good, it says it probably won’t kill you. She just got a good look into your soul. So congratulations, you’ll live a few more hours. With a tainted soul.” Roman’s sarcasm wasn’t helping her panic right now.

Blaire threw the car into park and stumbled from behind the wheel, then skidded and slid her way over the icy parking lot toward the trail that led to Winter’s Edge. Maybe he was there.

“I think you should leave,” Asher said from behind her.

“I’ve got that hint every time you’ve talked to me Asher, thank you. Surprise me and be nice instead.”

“I am! Fuck, kid, I’m trying to save your life.”

“I’m not a kid. I’m older than you.”

“How much older?” Roman asked, trailing his brother.

“I’m thirty! This is my birthday trip, but everyone is ruining this!”

“Whoa, you look hot for an old lady.”

“Stop talking!” she yelled over her shoulder.

“I thought old ladies were supposed to be sweet,” Roman muttered. Stupid Roman with the stupid smile in his voice.

She wanted to hurt him with words. "Odine said you two might be evil," she said with a prim little "hmm" at the end for good measure.

"Odine's full of shit," Asher said from right beside her. His legs were longer, and he passed her. For some reason that pissed Blaire off even more, so she swished her hips and pushed her legs to keep up.

"I'm a little bit evil," Roman admitted.

"Roman, shut up," Asher gritted out.

"So is Asher. He just likes to pretend he's not. We like to do bad things."

"Stop lumping me in with you," Asher spat out over his shoulder. "We're nothing alike." Asher walked faster, and Blaire gritted her teeth and speed-walked to keep up.

He cast her a frown and went even faster.

Blaire took off running, but Asher and Roman blurred past her and disappeared into the woods, and now Roman's laughter was echoing everywhere.

"I think I hate you," she called, slowing to a jog, and then to a pouty walk.

"Ugh, what an evil thing to say," Roman said from somewhere up ahead. "Don't get lost Princess Human. These woods are haunted."

Blaire grimaced and looked around the darkening woods, then picked up her speed walking again. At least the trail was easy to follow thanks to the fresh boot prints in the snow. A few minutes more, and she made it to the clearing right in front of Winter's Edge. There was a parking lot on one side, so there had to be another road leading into here. Next time she was driving, especially if the woods were haunted. Two days ago, she hadn't believed in that stuff, but werewolves and witches had skewed her view of the entire world now.

Asher and Roman were waiting outside the door, leaned up against the log building like they'd been there for hours. Annoying.

"I'm calling a pack meeting," she muttered as she shoved open the door.

"You can't call a pack meeting," Asher gritted out. "A, you aren't an alpha, and B, we aren't a fucking pack. We're three rogues and a human."

"Princess Human," Roman corrected, following Blaire inside. "I like her. She's feisty and yells at everyone. She's fun to piss off. I kind of want to keep her, like a human pet."

Asher huffed a pissed-off sound. "Keep her all

you want. Die with her and Gentry for all I care. I'm out of here as soon as we dump the old man's ashes."

"I can hear everything you are saying," she muttered.

"You can?" Roman asked with his face all scrunched up. "I thought humans couldn't hear hardly anything."

"Seriously?" she asked, giving him the dirtiest face she could muster. "Are all werewolves this judgmental?"

"Yes," Asher and Roman both muttered in unison.

Fantastic. "Gentry?"

"Yeah, back here," Gentry called from the kitchen.

The Striker brothers hung back as she made her way around the bar top and through the kitchen door. She hadn't been in here before, but it looked nothing like the main room. This was all stainless-steel countertops and matching double ovens, stoves, and even dual microwaves. There was a walk-in fridge on the far wall. Gentry had just entered through the back door with a huge rolling trashcan he must have just emptied in the dumpster outside.

He looked exhausted, but his lips curved up into a smile immediately when he saw her. "Hey," he murmured, approaching her slow, like he didn't want to startle her.

"I did something bad," she murmured, bracing for his reaction.

Gentry just leaned into her though, hugging her tight. He didn't say anything, just swayed them side to side. Something was wrong. Blaire could feel it in her chest.

"Are you okay?" she asked.

Gentry lifted her up to sit on the counter then pulled her against him. He dipped his lips to her neck and pressed them there, let them linger until he finally sighed and said, "I'm better now. It was just a long day."

"Your dad?"

Gentry's attention flickered to an urn that sat on the counter against the wall. "I picked up his ashes today. Blaire, I think I let him down."

She eased back and cupped his cheeks. He'd shaved, so she could see every beautiful, sharp angle. "You didn't. You were out there living your life. If he wanted your help, he would've asked."

"He did ask, though. He asked me to stay and take on the pack."

"When?"

"On my eighteenth birthday. He was tired. He wanted to train me to take over, and I left instead."

Gentry glanced at the door, and when she followed his gaze, Roman and Asher were there, leaning their backs against the counter like they'd been there the whole time. Both had their eyes downcast, but she could see the gold and silver from here.

"I never understood why he didn't ask Asher," Roman said. "I mean, I get why he didn't ask me. I would hate being an alpha, but Asher's the oldest, the biggest, the most dominant. He always was. He wanted it. He was trainable, coachable. He worked to please Dad—"

"Enough," Asher demanded. "He didn't ask because he didn't ask. Drop it."

Roman stared at Asher a few moments too long, then huffed a disgusted breath. "Fine. We'll act just like we did when we were kids then. Nobody talk about anything serious, just keep everything fucking buried until it festers and ruins us all."

"That's not how I remember it when we were kids," Gentry said, holding Blaire's hips tighter. He had his chin tucked to his chest, but he was meeting Asher's challenging gaze.

Asher crossed his arms over his chest, bulging out his biceps as his eyes filled with fury. "Your memories aren't real, Gentry."

"Bullshit. You mean they don't count."

"That, too! You were favored. You were king. I was nothing. Dad wouldn't even look at me. Do you know how it feels to devote your life to pleasing a man who finds you completely and utterly fucking invisible? He didn't see Roman either, but Roman didn't need to be seen by him."

"That's not true," Roman warned.

"You didn't! You made a joke of everything. You always had a smile on your face, always made people laugh, were always happy like you didn't give a single shit about what was happening in our fucking house. You and I were in the corner in the darkest shadow the entire first eighteen years of our life. You want to talk about something real, Roman? How about you didn't give a shit when we were kicked out of the pack, and I still hate you for not being angry."

"I was angry—"

"You weren't—"

"I was and I still am, Asher! I just don't deal with anger the way you do! Fuck! I hate this place," Roman yelled, gripping the back of his hair. "I didn't want to come back. I didn't want to do this. I hate that I hate my brothers, and I hate that you both hate me. I wanted normal! That's all I ever fuckin' wanted."

"Well, blame that one," Asher gritted out, jerking his chin to Gentry.

"Oh, you think I wanted to be the favored?" Gentry asked. "Really? I was left out of everything with you two. You banded together. You talk about being in the shadows, but you put me there, too, on the opposite side of the room as you two. Always talking about me like I was this spoiled little shit, like I wanted the extra attention from Dad. Like I wanted the pack! Asher, I thought you would take it. I looked up to you. I thought if I was quiet enough, you would just come in there and take it and save me from all the shit I didn't want to do. From all the pressure. I wasn't some prodigal son. Dad built me up that way, and so did the pack, but I wasn't feeding it. I wasn't reveling in it. It wasn't some warm place to bask in. It was fucking cold and lonely. I hated it because it separated me from the two of you. I wanted to be with you. Three amigos. You wanted normal, Roman? Well, so did I! Why do you think I left when you two got kicked out of the pack? Huh? It wasn't to chase some easy life. I went through hell when I left here. Guilt hell. Poverty hell. Lonely hell. But for me it was worth it because I was pissed that you weren't going to be a part of the pack. And if you weren't there, I didn't want anything to do with it. I still don't. Everyone preached about how it was my destiny to take over, but it isn't. I would rather stay rogue the rest of my life than make the two of you hate me even more. As long as you two stay rogue...I stay rogue."

Asher was shaking his head, staring at the wall, teeth gritted so hard his jaw clenched. "Not that I care about you—at all—but you need to leave town, Gentry. You and Blaire both. Now. Tonight."

"What? No, I still have loose ends to tie up. Dad's ashes still need to be spread. This place isn't going to clean up itself, and you assholes have been zero help."

"We'll do it," Roman said, but he was looking at Blaire with some warning look she didn't understand.

Was she supposed to talk now? This felt like

family business.

"Okay, spread the old man's ashes." Asher strode for the urn and hooked an arm around it as he passed, didn't slow at all and headed straight for the back door.

"What are you doing?" Gentry yelled as he bolted after him. He and Roman nearly got stuck in the door trying to get to Asher, but that could be blamed on their shoulders, which were roughly the width of a broad side of a barn.

"Get off me," Gentry growled, shoving Roman.

Blaire sprinted after them, but Asher was doing something really bad. He was standing ten yards into the woods and had jerked the lid off the urn.

Gentry bolted for him. "Wait, he wanted to be buried by the river."

"He loved this place more than his family, so..." Asher began to dump a cloud of light silver ashes into the snow just as Gentry and Roman reached him.

"Fuck, Asher, stop!" Gentry yelled, grabbing for the urn. "We're supposed to say something nice and invite Odine."

Asher wrestled out of Gentry and Roman's grip, spewing clouds of ash from the ceramic container.

"Oh my God," Roman said, dropping to his knees and coughing as he speed-crawled away. "I've got Dad in my throat." He gagged and started shoveling snow into his mouth and scrubbing his tongue.

"Goddammit, Asher, this isn't the way we were supposed to do it!" Gentry yelled.

"Funerals are for the living," Asher said, chucking the urn at a tree like a football. It exploded into a cloud of leftover ashes and shards of ceramics. "Dad would just be happy we were all here to witness it."

"Odine wasn't here," Gentry yelled, stripping out of his ash-smattered jacket like it was on fire. "And she was his big secret, I don't know…favorite fuck or something. He would've wanted her here!"

Wait, Odine was their late father's…mate? He was the wolf she'd talked about losing?

Asher spat in the snow. "Well, Dad's favorite fuck outed Blaire in front of the pack in town today. You want to scoop some of these ashes up and call her over? I don't. Fuck her. She just killed the both of you. Unless you run."

"What?" Gentry asked, scrubbing snow on his hands, washing away ashes. He turned a blazing green gaze on Blaire. "Are you okay?"

"I'm fine, but your step-monster is a lunatic. She talked about stirring up the hive and making you step up, making your brothers stop being evil."

"Again, we're not evil!" Asher clipped out, his eyes so silver they were almost white.

"Well, you just dumped your dad's ashes all over your brothers, so I guess we can just agree to disagree," Blaire muttered.

"Well…at least I'm not banging outside of my species!" Asher yelled.

"She's a human, not a hamster. Fuck you," Gentry said to Asher as he kicked his dirty jacket toward Winter's Edge.

"Fuck you, too!" Asher said.

"Fuck you both," Roman said from where he was still scrubbing his mouth with snow.

"You three are a disaster," Blaire murmured tiredly as she stared at the ashes that painted the snow.

Roman spat in the snow and leaned back on his folded legs. "Well, now we can all survive if we just get out of town in time to avoid the Bone-Ripper Pack."

That sounded terrifying. "Bone-Rippers?" Blaire

asked in a much smaller voice than she'd intended.

"I'm leaving," Asher muttered as he walked past. "See you idiots at the next funeral."

Gentry was staring at Blaire, his eyes sparking like green fire. He exhaled deeply through clenched teeth. "I'm not leaving." He'd said it at normal volume, but it sounded loud in the silence of the evening woods.

"What?" Asher said, turning a furious gaze on his brother.

"If you saw the pack, you would understand. I'm not running. I can't." He looked at his brothers. "You two know as well as I do that Rhett will drive the people here into the ground. Not just the pack either, but the humans in this town. So they found out about me and Blaire. I made the decision already that I wouldn't be able to hide her. Wolf won't let me shove her in a den. He's proud of her. *I'm* proud of her. So, she's human…" Gentry shrugged one shoulder up and arched his eyebrow in an I-don't-give-a-single-fuck expression.

"Rules, Gentry," Asher barked out.

"Rules are for packs, Asher. I like her. I want her. Wolf won't have anyone else. She's human. Sucks. I wish she was a wolf, but she isn't."

"Rhett will put out a kill order," Roman said from where he sat in the snow.

"Rhett can *try* to kill me." Gentry's voice was low and growly, like a demon's voice. He stood with his back to the dark woods, fists clenched, shoulders bulging against his tight sweater. "I'm not Dad."

"He killed Dad in an alpha challenge," Asher said, like that made murder all right.

Gentry shook his head slowly. "I don't think so. I think he killed him human. I think it was a coup to take the pack and done in the shadows."

"What?" Roman barked out, horror etched into his face.

Asher muttered a curse and paced away, then back. "Do you have proof?"

"Not yet."

Asher linked his hands behind his neck and shook his head for a long time as he stared off into the woods, but at last, he said, "So what's your plan, Favorite?"

"To take back the town."

Asher and Roman let off twin laughs that echoed through the forest. "As a rogue?"

"No. As three rogues."

The smiles fell from both Asher and Roman's faces.

"Nope. Not doing this. Uh-uh. I'm leaving," they both said, stumbling over each other's words. Roman stood and strode for the front of Winter's Edge.

"Stay just until we can get a new alpha in place. Just until we can avenge Dad." Gentry grabbed Blaire's hand as he passed and murmured, "This involves you now, Trouble. Come on."

"And who do you suggest we put on the throne of the Bone-Rippers?" Asher asked over his shoulder.

"Tim. Nelda. Hell, Mila would be better than Rhett."

"Oh, good, a submissive alpha," Roman said sarcastically as he lengthened his stride. "She'll love that job."

"Okay stop!" Gentry demanded.

Roman and Asher gave matching snarls and turned on Gentry. They looked terrifying, but when Blaire looked up at Gentry, he looked wilder than all of them. Profile rigid, eyes glowing, face twisted in some fearsome look she'd never seen.

"The Bone-Rippers will be at the Four Horsemen

tonight. Eleven o'clock, and they should be gathered. One hour there and then make your decision whether to stay or go, and I won't stop you. I won't try to persuade you. I'll let you go back to your lives, and we can go right back to the way it was. Just...give me one hour before you decide."

Asher didn't give an answer. Instead, he let off a fierce growl, turned on his heel, and made his way down the trail that led back to the cabins.

Roman watched him leave, scratching his bearded jaw in irritation. Finally, he ghosted Gentry a glance and muttered, "You're buying." He made to leave but turned and jammed his finger at Gentry. "And I drink *a lot*." And then he followed Asher's boot prints and disappeared into the woods.

Gentry leaned heavily against a tree and scrubbed his hands over his face. He let off a sigh, and his eyes dimmed. He looked haunted like the woods that surrounded him. "I worked so hard to get away from this place and stay gone. If I told you what I really want, you would run."

Blaire squared up to him, her boots sinking in the ankle-deep snow. With just a moment of hesitation, she wrapped her arms around his middle.

"I'd rather you talk to me than not. That goes for always. I don't like all the secrets. I like knowing what's going on. I like knowing you."

Gentry leaned down and kissed her gently, stroked his fingertip down her cheek, then eased back and pressed his lips to her forehead. "You have this safe life back home. You could leave now and nothing bad would happen to you. I know you would be okay. You could find a normal man, with normal human problems, and be happy. But when I think about letting you go, everything in me buckles against it, Trouble. And the selfish monster in me wants you to stay here and go through this fight with me, bond to me, fall for me, and I want to make it to where you can never leave. Where you would never want to. I want to make you so happy you can't imagine your life without me in it. Something's wrong with me."

"It's not selfish, Gentry," she whispered, sliding her hands around the back of his neck and standing on her tiptoes to hug him. "I want those same things. All of them. I can't explain it, but you feel important. No, that's not even a big enough word. You feel crucial. To me, to my growth as a person, to my happiness, all of it." Before she could change her mind, she blurted out, “I called a realtor about selling my house.”

“What?” he asked, easing her back to arm’s length. “So you can move here?”

“No! Oh, my gosh, no. That makes me sound like a stalker.”

“Oh.” Gentry frowned.

“Wait, is that what you want? You would want me to move to Rangeley? We’ve known each other for—”

“Don’t. Don’t point it out. It’ll make me feel even more selfish.”

“No, I am selling the house I shared with my ex-husband. I’ve been clinging to it. Clinging to the idea of him. I failed big-time in my marriage, and it was scary to move on and start over. So, selling my house is a really big step for me. It’s my goodbye to my old life, and I have you to thank for it. You make me feel ready to move on.”

“Good.” Gentry gave a cocky smile and slid his hands under her jacket to grip her hips. “I’m proud of you.”

“I like that you say stuff like that.”

“Well, I like your freckles.”

"I like your wolf-eyes."

His grin turned wicked, and before she knew it, she was tossed over his shoulder like a log. He smacked her ass hard enough to sting. "I like that."

"I like that you give me erotica books to read."

"Yeah? Did you read Chapter Four?"

"Part of it. Odine interrupted me mid-imaginary coitus."

"Ugh, she's the worst," he teased.

"She cock-blocked my imagination."

"I'll reenact the rest of that scene for you," he said in a growly, sexy voice.

"Wait, really?" she asked low, arching up so she could see his face. "I would really like whatever that entails."

"Well, not down to the letter," he said, letting her slide to his front and wrap her legs around his hips. He kept walking like she was no burden at all. "Desmund gave Sheela a claiming mark, and those are a no-no with real life werewolves. A claiming mark from me would kill you."

"Wait, what? Kill me, you say? What?"

Gentry frowned and settled her on her feet, then slid his big strong hand around hers and kept walking without missing a beat. "I won't ever do that. I won't bite you. You're safe with me. Wolf wouldn't allow it. I know he wouldn't."

"Wolf?"

"He's separate. It's not supposed to be like that, but it's just how I am. There's human me and Wolf."

"So when you were sitting in the middle of the road today..."

"I was barely present. You were meeting Wolf. For him, you're it. You're everything."

"And for you?"

He flashed her a serious, green-eyed glance and murmured, "Same. You said you want to know everything."

"I do. The good the bad and the ugly. Lay it on me, wolf-man."

He chuckled. "True story, I've never talked to anyone as openly as I talk to you. It's a relief. I was kind of glad you found out last night and saw Wolf today. Feels good not having to hide from you. I've been on my own so long, it's so damn nice to share things with someone I trust."

"You trust me?" she asked in a mushy high-pitched squeak.

Gentry grabbed her ass hard and shook it a couple times as he growled and nipped her neck gently. "I showed you my wolf, Trouble. That is *the biggest* sign of trust with my people. Plus, you're fun to fuck."

She giggled as he sucked on her neck. "You have a filthy mouth."

"You like it," he accused. "You smell like you want sex when I talk how I want to you." He kissed her hard and ran his hand up the back of her sweater, unhooked her bra, then trailed his fingers to her front and slipped his palm under her loose bra and squeezed her breast gently. "Pretend you're a proper lady all you want. I like that. I like your cute clothes, your make-up all done up, and those fancy snow boots you lace up to your knees. I like that you try not to cuss, and that you use big words. But you're bad just for me, aren't you, Trouble?" he murmured against her throat. "You wear those sexy see-through panties that say you want me to make you feel good." When he slid his hand down the front of her jeans, Blaire arched back her head and gasped as he slid his finger into her. "I fucking love the way you react when I touch you. It's instant. You start shaking, and your heart starts pounding. I can hear it. Can smell you wanting me. Fills my senses and makes me crazy for you. Makes me lose my mind, and today was long, Trouble. I wanna lose my mind. Will you take it for a little while?"

"Fine, but I want something in return." She kissed his neck, and then sucked gently.

Gentry groaned out the word, "Anything."

"I want your heart to."

Gentry picked her up and held her close as he walked them toward the cabin. He leaned forward and whispered against her ear, "That was yours from the moment I saw you."

Butterflies flapped around in her stomach so hard she hunched into herself with the sensation and let off a happy sigh. And before she could stop her mouth, the words, "I think I love you," plopped out.

Mortified, she squeaked and buried her face against his shoulder.

He laughed and gathered her hair at the nape of her neck, then pulled her back gently and locked onto her with that striking gaze of his. "When was the last time you said that to a man?"

"My ex." Her cheeks were on fire. Right about

now, she could probably fry an egg on her face.

"And before that?"

Blaire shrugged. "No one before that. Met the ex when we were kids."

"So you're saying I'm only your second I love you."

She nodded and scrunched her face up into an embarrassed smile.

Gentry set her down outside her cabin's front door. He slid his hands down her arms, his fingertips making a zipping noise against the thick material of her winter coat. He intertwined his fingers with hers and leaned into her, kissed her so sweetly. Much sweeter than a man who had the devil in his smile should be able to. He disengaged with a soft smack and then cupped the back of her head and kissed her forehead, her closed eyes, the tip of her nose.

And then he whispered something that changed her life in a moment. "I love you too, Blaire. Before you, there was no one. You're the first and only."

FIFTEEN

Gentry loved her.

It hadn't been a slow build either. This burning light between them had been an explosive sensation that left Blaire breathless. Was this what love was supposed to be like? Was it the sudden realization of some other force in the universe shaped exactly like the hole in her heart? Was a connection like this supposed to be so instantaneous?

Gentry led her into the cabin by only her fingertips. She felt like she was floating. Last night had been incredible, but now she knew she wasn't just casual sex to him.

Everything.

She'd never been that for someone else before.

She'd been an add-on, but never everything. If this was what it was like bonding to a werewolf, she didn't mind what he was at all. It made no difference that he had Wolf inside of him. She adored them both. He and the animal were both hers to protect now.

Gentry turned at the bedroom door and walked backward, peeling off his shirt.

His six-pack flexed with the movement, his scars silver in contrast with his tanned skin. His deep V of muscle guided her attention right to his crotch. He lifted his chin and smirked as he undid his belt that rode low on his hips.

"Whoo," she sighed out, shaking her head in disbelief that he was hers.

He nodded and dragged his gaze to her jacket. "Your turn."

Oh, he wanted a strip-tease. There was a hundred percent chance she was about to turn him off indefinitely with her un-sexy moves, but she was game for anything if he would let loose his dang belt.

With a nervous laugh, she splayed her hands on his abs and pushed him backward until his back hit the wall closest to his bed. Gentry relaxed against it and waited, so she unzipped her jacket slowly and shrugged out of it. She pulled her sweater over her head, but it got hooked on her dangly earring. Blaire tried to be smoother, removed the earring and left it in the shirt, dropped the sweater on the ground, then removed her other earring in a rush. Gentry chuckled, and Blaire's cheeks heated slightly. If this was anyone else, she would've gotten super embarrassed and quit, but Gentry made it easy to be herself. That, and he was still rocking an obvious boner, so she wasn't doing that bad. The boots were next. She was clumsy, but he didn't seem to mind so long as she did her bending at the waist with her butt toward him. Socks and skinny jeans removed, she locked her arms on the bed and wiggled her see-through lace, hooker-red panty-clad butt at him with a laugh.

But Gentry wasn't smiling anymore. His eyes were trained on her backside, and that man looked hungry. As she moved to stand, he shoved off the wall and gently pushed her between the shoulder blades until she was back to resting her palms on the mattress.

He ran a light fingertip along her red lacy bra. "Did you match your lingerie for me today, Trouble?"

"Maybe," she said cheekily. "Or maybe I just

matched them for myself."

"Mmmm," he murmured, the sound tapering into a growl as he leaned his body over hers. He inhaled deeply at her neck and whispered, "Werewolves can sense a lie." He hooked a finger into the lace at her hip and rolled his erection against her ass. "Are these for me?"

Excitement zinged through her. "Yes," she said on a breath. "It's all for you."

Her bra went loose and fell around her wrists. There was the quick rattle of his zipper and, oh, this was happening fast now. The shuffle of clothes sounded, and then her panties slid down her thighs to her ankles. She kicked out of them—ungracefully of course—and gasped when he nudged her legs wider with his foot. He pushed her shoulder blades until she was resting on her elbows on the bed, ass up in the air. His hand was in her hair at the nape of her neck now, pulling gently, making her arch her back as he teased her with the head of his swollen cock. This had never been her favorite position, but Gentry was changing that quick.

He reached around her thigh and cupped her sex, ran his fingers through her folds and chuckled against the back of her neck. One bitey kiss, and he whispered, “I like how wet you get for me, Trouble.”

Words completely failed her. She wished she had something witty to say back, something that would turn him on, but all she managed was a helpless moan as he pushed his dick into her.

She was dizzy with how good he felt inside of her, stretching and filling her over and over. He sped up, and his thrusts became more powerful as he pushed her farther onto the bed. He released her hair, and then his hand was on her breast, squeezing hard, and his other arm was locked beside her ribs. His body was so powerful against hers as he thrusted over and over again.

She cried out at the peak of every stroke. He was so big she was on the verge of pain, but the pleasure overrode everything and fogged her mind. Suddenly, Gentry pulled out of her and rolled her onto her back, and then he was on her again, his abs flexing as he pushed into her.

Blaire wrapped her legs around his hips and clawed at his back as the pressure in her middle exploded outward. The orgasm came so hard and fast she didn’t even have time to cry out his name. All she could do was cling to him as he slammed into her. He paused as pulsing warm fluid flooded her, then reared back and bucked again—warmth, warmth, again and again, until neither one of them had anything left.

Blaire's entire body was shaking, but that was okay because Gentry was shaking, too. Such deep emotion welled up inside of her as she hugged him close and laid pecking kisses all over his neck and shoulder. God, she loved him. She loved the way he was protective and sweet, understanding and strong. She loved the way they fit together. She loved that he hadn't just finished without her and left her alone on the bed. He'd flipped her over when he was close and made sure she came with him.

"Gentry," she murmured, her heart overflowing.

"I know. I know," he chanted against her neck. "I can feel it."

"What?"

"I can feel how happy you are, Blaire. I can feel you."

A tear streamed out of the corner of her eye. Maybe that's what was happening to her, too. Maybe all this emotion wasn't only hers. "Is this… Are we okay?"

"Yeah," he said, cupping her neck and easing back. His eyes were glowing again, and his teeth looked sharper when he smiled, but at least he was smiling. "Bonds are only supposed to happen to werewolves. I thought…I thought we wouldn't have it." He shook his head, baffled. "I fucking love you, Blaire. I fucking *love* you," he murmured, closing his eyes tightly and resting his forehead on hers.

Another wave of potent emotion washed through her as she clung to him and cried as quietly as she could. She'd been so sad, utterly heartbroken, at the failure of her marriage, and then to find this? With Gentry?

But there was something more behind the joy and relief that was pulsing through her. Something dark. Something sad.

Confused, she pushed him back so she could look in his eyes when she asked, "What's wrong?"

Gentry looked away and rolled to the side, pulling her with him. He was quiet for so long, but this was Gentry's way. He didn't give himself easily, and if he was struggling with the words, it must've been important.

At last, he sighed and stroked her hair. "I'm not allowed to be with you—"

"I don't care about the rules—"

"I don't either except when it comes to your safety, Blaire. There are people in this town who would follow through with the punishment. Werewolves police themselves. My dad chose Odine, a human, and now he's..." *Dead.* "What if they found out about her, and that has something to do with his death? I can't risk the same thing happening to us. To you."

"But Odine is alive."

"Because she has black magic you wouldn't believe, Blaire. I saw some of it. I tasted it. Fuck, it nearly crippled me. She pulled the human out of me when I was Wolf, like it was nothing. She did it to my brothers, too. If the Bone-Rippers are smart, they won't mess with her. But you have no defense but me."

"But you can protect me."

"And I will. With my life, I'll make sure you're safe. But as much as I want you here, with me, where I can see you and touch you and make sure you're okay, Rangeley isn't safe for you. And what kind of man—what kind of mate—would I be if I kept you here?"

"Don't push me away, Gentry. Don't make me leave. I'm not ready."

"It's not forever. And nothing in me wants to do it except for this instinct to keep you safe. And right now, keeping you safe means keeping you away from all that is happening in this town."

Blaire flinched away from him and crossed her arms over her chest like a shield. "That's not how this is supposed to work. We're supposed to be a team. You're not supposed to say you love me and then push me away."

Yep, she was angry, but this was unexpected. She was supposed to have more time here with Gentry. Everything important suddenly felt like it was right here in Rangeley, and the thought of leaving when Gentry was headed right for the eye of whatever supernatural storm was brewing made her want to sink her claws in and stay.

She log-rolled out of bed and landed clumsily on her feet on the worn wooden floor. It was cold in here, and chills instantly took her body without Gentry's warmth, so she rushed for the bathroom and turned on the hot water in the shower.

"What are you doing?" Gentry asked.

"I'm getting ready for a night out on the town, because surely you don't expect me to leave tonight. It's late, snowy, and Roman broke my window. I'll freeze and die of frostbite."

Gentry let off a growl in the other room. "If I take you to the Four Horsemen tonight, will you promise to leave first thing in the morning?"

Hell no, but werewolves could sense lies, so she started singing that good-girl-gone-bad chorus and stepped into the steaming shower. Blaire closed her eyes and let the water rush over her hair, but startled when she felt Gentry's strong arms wrap around her waist. The scary predator in him made his movements silent.

He gently sucked her earlobe, then murmured, "I know what you're doing."

"Stalling?"

"Mmm hmm."

"I'll go when I'm ready to go."

He huffed a laugh and shook his head against her cheek. "I can make most people do what I want with a look, and then you come along and tell me 'no' on everything."

She rolled her back against him. "Not on everything."

"Will you leave in the morning?" he asked, his tone deadly serious.

With a sigh, Blaire turned in his arms and hugged his waist. For a few moments, she watched the water droplets racing down the contours of his muscular chest. She tried to imagine leaving but couldn't wrap her head around this being one of the last times they shared a moment like this. "No."

SIXTEEN

Blaire was going to be the death of him.

Death from acute stress.

And what could he do? He couldn't force her to leave. Wait, maybe he could. He could drive her cute, round ass to the airport himself. Nah, she would jump out at a stop sign. His woman was feisty.

"Motherfucker," he murmured, studying her rental car window. Roman's handprints had dented it enough that the window pane was now stuck inside the damn door. Laugh and joke all he wanted, Roman still had the same temper.

Asher, he barely recognized anymore. Not only was he bigger with a slew of new ink, he *felt* different, too. Even more dominant. Even quieter. Darker. More dangerous, and Gentry couldn't get a read on his thoughts at any given moment. Asher had one hell of a poker face now. Maybe he would show up to the Four Horsemen tonight, but probably not, as was evident from him currently shoving his duffle bag into the bed of his black-on-black Tundra.

Gentry shoved a piece of cardboard over Blaire's window and bit off a long piece of duct tape, then began to secure it. The snow was falling steadily, and the last thing she needed was a pile of the white stuff to sit in when they took it to the auto-body shop in the morning. He could fix a lot of things, but this was out of his wheel house. No, not just this. *Rangeley* was out of his wheel house. What the fuck was he doing here? He could rent this place or, hell, even sell it to some small business guru who would hopefully get it up and running again. And then he could follow Blaire to her hometown and give it a go at making her happy. Or if he couldn't manage that—and there were no guarantees because he'd never paired up before—at the very least, he could keep her safe. He could watch over her. He would be good at that. He'd trained his body for war all these years when he'd hunted the wild packs. Sure, the goal had always been to let as many survive as possible, and he'd saved a lot of wolves by taking out the problem animals instead of giving the ranchers free rein to annihilate entire packs, but he'd bled for that job. And in turn, he'd become more of a monster than his brothers or the Bone-Rippers realized.

But the Bone-Rippers were too uncertain right now for him to feel any comfort about Blaire being on the same continent with them.

Just like when he'd hunted the wild packs, it was easy to sense the problem animals. Rhett was top of that list, but who were his allies? Who had backed his play to take the pack? Gentry by no means had all the answers yet, and it would be a slow stalk until he had a better understanding of the new pack dynamics, but culling the bad wolf could potentially save the rest of the pack. Then he could leave Rangeley and hope for a life with Blaire without those pestering loose ends tripping him up.

He couldn't have a future with Blaire until he took care of his past.

And if she wanted to see the good, the bad, and the ugly, as she'd put it, maybe he should let her stay. Blaire had told him everything Odine had said while they were in the shower, so he knew without a shadow of a doubt that Blaire was on the Bone-Rippers' radar. Nothing happened in this town without the pack knowing about it.

They wouldn't try anything in a public bar, and Blaire was so damn charming maybe she could sway a few of the pack members into liking her. Cause some dissention in the ranks. "Stir up the hive" as Odine had put it. That witch had her reasons for causing trouble with the Bone-Rippers, and Gentry would keep an eye on that, but his reasons for creating a buzz were different. He wanted to watch reactions, watch loyalty lines, see who could be saved, see who needed to be protected, just like when he hunted the wild wolves that were preying on ranchers' livestock. Now he was going to hunt Rhett and unearth all the shit he'd done to steal the throne of the Bone-Rippers, formerly the Striker Pack. Formerly his father's pack. Formerly a good, town-protecting pack.

The door to Blaire's cabin banged closed, and she jogged down the stairs looking like a million bucks. Her dark jeans clung to her curves like a second skin, and she was zipping up her jacket over a sky-blue sweater that made her eyes look jungle green. She'd smoked up her eyes with dark make-up and wore her red-gold hair in sexy waves that were long enough to reach the bottom of those perfect tits of hers. God, he would never get tired of looking at her, but he had to play it cool. If a woman like her found out just how obsessed he was, she would run for the hills.

Blaire was tough as nails, and had a mouth to match, but her divorce had hurt her deeply and made her a little skittish at times, which is why her declaration that she wasn't leaving him meant so damn much. She'd buckled her legs against any forward motion the second he'd suggested her going back to her hometown early. Down to his soul, he respected the hell out of this woman.

She flashed him a bright white smile and ran the last steps, flung her arms around him, and jumped. His clumsy girl nearly took them to the ground, but Gentry was quick at recovering.

"God, you weigh a ton," he joked, pretending to drop her.

"Stop!" she exclaimed. "You'll give me a complex."

"About what?" he asked, gripping her ass with

both hands and jiggling it. This was making him want a round two at taking her from behind. "I think your ass is my favorite part to grab. Your boobs are fucking tens too, but this ass, Trouble. I want to bite it."

"Okay, never mind on the complex, I'm good, butt-man, and no biting because I want to survive."

"Not a break-the-skin nip, but a little...love bite."

"Let's make-out," she said with a naughty grin.

Gentry laughed and kissed the mango gloss off her lips. No one had ever amused him like she did. She was playful in a way he'd never sensed in anyone else. He could've stayed here all night, pressing her against the rental car, lost in exploring her mouth and body, but after a few minutes, Blaire began to shiver.

Gentry eased back and frowned. "Are you cold?"

"Well, yeah! It's freezing out here, and I'm not a werewolf."

"Oh." Being a human probably sucked. "Okay, we need to have a serious discussion about saying that word in town. Werewolves aren't out to the public, obviously, and hinting that they exist will get you—"

"Let me guess," she said sarcastically. "It'll get me killed." She lowered to her feet, pitched to the side, righted herself as he chuckled at her lack of grace, and then she pretended to zip her lips. "Don't worry, Chaos. Your million secrets are safe with me. Although I did tell my best friend you are an animal in the sack," she murmured, making her way toward his truck, which was already turned on and warming up for her. "I think it was the filthiest thing I've ever said to someone. Ashlyn said she was proud of me for getting laid, but I couldn't bring myself to tell her how much more it is that we're doing. Is it weird that I want to keep what we're building to myself for a while?" she asked, turning her pretty gaze on him at the passenger's side door.

"No, not weird. I like the thought of having you all to myself for a bit, too. Well…I guess it's different because you've met all my family now."

"And they don't approve."

"Does that bother you?" he asked, helping her into his truck.

"Heck yeah, it bothers me! My mom is going to love you, and Ashlyn will, too, but your brothers will probably never accept me on account of my human-ness and all. Which, by the way, is ridiculous and super judgmental."

"So you're judging their judgmental-ness."

"Precisely," she said with a megawatt grin that left his heart stuttering in his chest.

The most beautiful woman in the entire world was sitting in the front seat of his beater truck, smiling at him like he wasn't a monster, even though she'd seen both sides of him.

"When you're thirty, I'll be thirty-four," she said out of the blue as he pulled out of the parking lot between the cabins.

He tossed her a grin because she had to be joking, but she looked back at him with wide, worried eyes.

Gentry asked, "Does the age difference bother you?"

"I'm afraid it will eventually bother you. You're young and all muscled up and have tattoos and scars and zero face-wrinkles, and you can have any woman you want, Gentry. Literally, anyone you want. I'm practically a mummy," she muttered.

That was ridiculous and made him laugh out loud. "Woman, I'm a damn werewolf, and you accepted that in about three seconds. I've given zero thoughts to you being older than me. You fit me fine the way you are. You aren't a mummy. You're perfect."

"Swear it doesn't bother you?"

Gentry shook his head, pulled her hand into his lap, and pressed her palm against the bulge in his pants, still raging thanks to their little make-out session a minute ago. "I swear. Besides, if anyone saw us out together, they would assume I'm older than you."

"Liar and flatterer. You are just trying to secure yourself a blow job."

"I'm serious. I'm a foot taller than you and quieter. That could pass as more mature in some circles, Trouble. No one is going to care that you're robbing the cradle."

She swatted him, and he winced like it hurt so she wouldn't feel weak.

"Oh, this is my favorite song," she said, turning up the radio.

He arched his eyebrow and tried not to laugh. "It's a condom commercial. See? I'm more mature."

"I don't know what you're talking about," she murmured, her cute little chin lifted in the air as she pulled a pair of pink mittens onto her hands. The color matched her rosy cheeks. She belted out the entire jingle to the condom commercial. He loved everything about her.

"Are you happy?" he asked suddenly. Her answer mattered to him a terrifying amount.

Blaire slid her hand into his and rested it on his thigh. "I'm happy with you. I'm happy to be here. I'm happy to be moving on with my life, with my friends and family, and with my job. I'm not happy that you're taking on this crazy town by yourself. When we left, Roman and Asher didn't look like they were coming. Asher was packing his car up to leave, and Roman was sitting on the porch in his underwear drinking what I'm pretty sure was my last bottle of red wine. He wasn't even using a cup. And he didn't smile at me when I waved. He looked angry."

So, she had seen that bit. Apparently, Asher had convinced his youngest brother not to get involved. Fucking annoying how they always banded together, and Gentry was always the odd-brother out, but what could he do about it?

"I don't want you to do this alone," Blaire finished quietly. "Maybe we should call Odine."

"Not until I know her intentions. I don't like her

interest in you, or whatever fate she thinks is in store for me, and I don't like that she is manipulating us into place for some agenda she doesn't feel like sharing. I'm out on Odine. It's a bad idea to trust a witch, Trouble. Always remember it. That's a sure-fire way to breathe your last breath sooner. And her burning your hair? I don't want her anywhere near you."

"Why is it so dark out here?" Blaire asked, right as his instincts were wondering the same thing.

Gentry was halfway to town, dark woods on either side of the road, but there were usually bright streetlights leading the way toward Main Street. Gentry leaned forward, looked up at the dark light on the left, and narrowed his eyes at the shattered glass and bulb. "What the fuck is going on?" he murmured. "Those were fine yesterday."

A howl lifted on the breeze, and Gentry slammed on the brakes as a shadowy figure appeared out of the woods and threw something across the road. The strip of nails glistened in the moonlight right before the truck skidded sideways over them.

The popping of the tires was loud, and he reached across to Blaire, held her in place as the truck went up on two wheels. Her scream filled his head and did something awful to Wolf.

The truck went up on two wheels and rolled. "Hold on!" he yelled as they crashed and landed upside down. Everything slowed. Maybe it was shock or denial that caused time to drag, but Gentry was thrown forward against his seatbelt, and there was such terror in Blaire's eyes as the windows shattered inward. He watched her lips as she screamed, and everywhere tiny fragments of glass rained. And then time resumed as the truck rocked upside down and settled.

Another howl filled the air, and another. These weren't his brothers' voices that called him to war this time. This was Tim, Nelda, and even Mila. This was the Bone-Rippers promising pain. Fury blasted through his veins as he cradled Blaire's head from where it was resting on the roof of the car, right on top of glass. Blood was streaming from a cut on her forehead, and her wide, frightened eyes were locked on him. She was panting so fast she would pass out soon if he didn't settle her. Out of the broken front windshield, Gentry could see Rhett stride from the woods in nothing but a pair of jeans, a ripped-up T-shirt, and unlaced combat boots, like he was ready for the Change. He stalked toward the truck, a feral smile stretching his face as he stepped over a lane of snow.

Fuck. Gentry strained his hand against the roof of the car to give himself room to unbuckle. He had to get Blaire out of here. She was a sitting duck strapped to his truck like this, and there was smoke coming from the engine. The buckle clicked, and he hit the ground hard. There wasn't enough room to move easily, but he had desperation pushing him.

"It's okay, baby," he murmured. "I'm gonna get you out of here."

Blaire was crying, and her whole body was shaking. She'd probably never been in a wreck like this. She smelled like fear, and inside of him Wolf howled to be released. He was going to rip Rhett's throat out, but first, he had to take care of his mate.

Her seatbelt was jammed. Too much pressure on it maybe, but he didn't have time for this. No more hiding his strength from her. Blaire was about to see the darkness he was capable of anyway. Gentry ripped through her seatbelt with little effort and cradled her fall so she wouldn't cut herself on the shattered glass more than she already had. She had a dozen cuts on her face. Every drop of her blood that spilled, Gentry would take a hundred more from Rhett.

Blaire's window was crushed into an odd shape they would never escape from, so Gentry pulled her as carefully as he could toward his side. Gritting his teeth, he kicked his mangled door open and pulled her from the wreckage. The scent of smoke, gasoline, blood, and fur filled the air.

The wolves were still howling, getting closer, closing in, and Gentry was out of time. He rushed Blaire to the middle of the road and settled her on her feet. "Nothing's broken?" he asked frantically, gripping her shoulders, her arms, her ribs.

"N-no. Gentry, what's happening?"

A hunt was happening, but he didn't want to scare her even more. Blaire was the prey, but the pack would have to go through him to get to her. "I'm gonna Change." He cast a quick glance at Rhett, who was too fucking close to his mate now. "I'm gonna Change, and you're gonna run. Run back to Hunter Cove. I'll cover you."

Blaire's chest was heaving, and she looked around at the moonlit woods, now teaming with the

Bone-Ripper Pack. “I’m scared.”

“Shhhh,” Gentry murmured, cupping her cheeks to drag her attention back to him. “Look at me. Listen to me. No matter what happens, Wolf will take care of you.” He leaned in and kissed her hard and then ripped away. “Run, Blaire.”

SEVENTEEN

Gentry was bleeding, cut up bad from the glass. He hadn't protected himself during the crash, but had thrown his arm over her lap instead and kept Blaire pinned against the seat. She hadn't even stretched the seatbelt, and then he'd ripped right through it like he was pulling apart two paper towels.

Gentry was a lot stronger than she'd realized, but she could see the wolves, and there were many. Contrasting with the blue moon wilderness backdrop, most of the predators were differing shades of gray, but two were black. All had their teeth bared. All had their attention trained on her and Gentry.

How could Wolf protect her from all of these monsters and survive?

Trust me.

His blazing green eyes were begging her trust, and behind him, a dark-haired man in unlaced boots was striding toward them faster and faster.

"Run, Blaire," Gentry demanded, his voice gone dead. The look on his face was terrifying in the moment before he turned away from her and peeled off his shirt.

"Oh, my gosh," she said in a shaking voice as she bolted in the direction of Hunter Cove.

Nothing hurt yet. Warmth was streaming down her jawline, and she smelled like pennies, but the adrenaline was covering up the pain right now. The limp, though…the limp she couldn't help. It was slowing her down. Gritting her teeth, Blaire pushed herself harder and faster.

Gentry had promised he would get her out of here, but she hadn't missed it. He hadn't promised he would make it out. If she did just as he said and was really fast, perhaps he could be okay, too.

Gunfire filled the air, and she ducked with a scream. But when she turned around, she realized it wasn't guns at all but Gentry's bones breaking and reshaping in an instant. His charcoal gray wolf shook his head hard as he charged a big gray wolf with light points. They were a match in size, both huge.

Blaire kept running as she watched them over her shoulder in horror. They clashed so hard she felt the powerful vibrations in the air. The wolves in the woods were following her though, closing in, angling toward her, and now the leader, a black wolf, was right on the edge of the road.

One bite and she was dead. They were so *fast.*

"Gentry!"

And he was there beside her for just a moment before he charged the black wolf. A gray wolf attacked his back end, and then another joined the pile. She wanted to scream. She wanted to find a log in the woods and take it to them all like a baseball bat, but Gentry was the bone-ripper here. He shredded them, and not one at a time. She'd never seen such violence in all her life, hadn't realized what the man she loved was capable of.

His green eyes flashed at her as he slammed the black wolf against a tree in the woods. *Run, Blaire.*

She pushed her legs even faster, but she was still trailing three wolves, who were taking their time to attack. It was as if they were playing with her, or letting her tire herself out. The big gray one Gentry had fought first was loping along the road beside her, his eyes a dead and icy blue. His neck was streaming blood, making a trail of red in the snow, but he didn't seem bothered the injury. Blaire was slipping where the ice was thick, and it was slowing her down. Her leg was throbbing, her heartbeat was pounding against her chest, her lungs hurt from chugging the cold air, and every muscle in her body was twitching with exhaustion. Behind her, there was a resounding boom, and she ducked as heat blasted against her skin. A quick glance behind showed Gentry's truck in flames, lighting up the night.

When she turned back, the big gray wolf was right there. He snapped his teeth too close to her hand, and she pulled it away just a millisecond before he broke her skin. Blaire locked her legs against the ice and skidded onto her backside because there was a line of wolves blocking the road right in front of her. Her tailbone felt like it had blasted up into her throat, but there was no time for recovery. She scrambled up and away from the gray wolf who was herding her into the center of a loose circle of wolves.

And then Gentry was there, circling her tightly,

attention drifting from one wolf to the other. He tossed back his head and let off a loud howl. It was short, but so loud it hurt. Blaire hunched her shoulders and covered her ears as she searched frantically for a hole big enough to escape through. She hadn't been fast enough, and now she and Gentry were both easy targets.

He went after a black wolf who drifted too close but didn't engage before he bolted back to her and placed himself between her and Big Gray.

Blaire could clearly see the pack dynamics in play. The others were drawing Gentry away from her one by one, ducking closer and tempting him to lock onto them, while Big Gray paced closer.

A distant howl rose into the air, followed directly by another, and the effect on the pack was instant. All heads lifted and drifted in the direction of the woods where the haunting notes had come from. Ears were all erect, and Big Gray snarled, baring blood-stained teeth. The woods were alive with movement and glowing eyes as two monster wolves, much bigger than the others, sprinted toward them. One was black, but not like the other wolves. He was demon black with white eyes, while the other was gray mottled with brown and white with eyes the color of the sun.

Asher and Roman were here.

Gentry kept his focus on the pack, and when one ducked in with determination, he had no choice but to engage.

Big Gray let off a deep bark, and the pack lunged as one for her and Gentry. Blaire screamed as the two closest wolves' sharp teeth sank into her jacket and yanked her arm so hard she slammed to the ground. The sound of snarling was so loud now, and all around her was war. The Strikers were ripping into the pack with a vengeance, and the snow was being painted with crimson. But it was the two wolves on her that kept her attention. Both were a mottled gray color. They would've been beautiful if not for the horrifying looks of violence on their faces. It didn't matter that Blaire was fighting and hitting and kicking as hard and as furiously as she could. Their bites pierced through her clothes, and the first puncture of teeth was agony. The second was less, and so were the third and the fourth, and finally the pain ran together until it dulled suddenly. There was no point in screaming now, so she let the scratchy sound die in her throat.

Both wolves were ripped off her by Roman and Asher as Gentry battled Big Gray. The other wolves were scattering into the woods, limping, bleeding, escaping. The Strikers stood like sentries beside her as her mate snarled and bit and tore into the alpha of the Bone-Rippers.

Did he know her life was over yet?

Did Asher understand in this form? Did Roman?

Tears streamed down her cheeks. They were the only warm things about her. Inside her body, her blood had chilled to ice, stretching like clawed, dead fingers from the seeping bite-marks on her arms until it reached her chest, her stomach, her legs.

Gentry had pinned Big Gray, his teeth on his throat, poised to shred his neck and end his life, but Asher bolted forward and blasted into Gentry. Why? Why not let him end this? Why not let him avenge their dad? Avenge her?

Something big passed between Asher and Gentry with a look, and they both allowed Big Gray to drag his broken body toward the woods.

Blaire didn't feel well. The woods were beginning to spin around her, and she swayed where she sat. A cold sweat broke out all over her body, and she could feel a poisonous fog filling each vein. She looked down at her shredded arms. *Red, red, now I'm dead.*

"Gentry," she whispered weakly.

He looked over at her, locked his gaze on hers, and then dragged those firey green eyes down her body to her offered arms.

She wanted to say she was sorry. Sorry she hadn't run fast enough, sorry she hadn't given him more of a chance to save them, sorry she'd been weak, sorry she hadn't left when he'd asked her to. She wanted to say sorry she was ending them too soon. Her heart was breaking. Nothing was fair. All she could do was close her eyes against the spinning woods as she fell backward into the snow.

When she opened her eyes, the glowing blue moon was there, full and low in the cloudy sky. And then something even more beautiful was there, leaning over her, agony written into his face.

"No," Gentry whispered.

Gentry cradled her body against his chest as he shook his head in denial.

"Call the witch," Asher said low.

"Man, she can't do anything for her!" Roman said from where he paced right on the edge of her vision. "Fucking black magic, Asher? Really? She'll turn Blaire into one of those zombie wolves you imagined in the woods, and that's if Blaire's lucky. You'll owe a blood-debt to a witch, Gentry. Maybe Blaire will survive the bites."

"Three percent, Roman. That's the odds for a woman." Gentry stood slowly with Blaire in his arms, his eyes empty as he walked her up the road toward Hunter Cove.

So strong.

He acted as if her dead weight was nothing.

Dead weight.

Dead.

"Gentry!" Roman said. "Odine can't save her!"

"Shut the fuck up," Asher snarled out in a voice more wolf than man. "Zombie wolf or no, at least she would have a chance at living. Open your eyes, Roman. They're bonded. If she dies, Gentry dies."

"That's not possible. She's human!"

"Yeah, well, witches and werewolves aren't supposed to exist," Gentry barked out over his shoulder. "Anything's possible." He looked down at

Blaire and repeated that last part through gritted teeth. "Anything's possible. Do you hear me, Blaire? Don't quit on me."

"You'll die, too?" she asked weakly.

"No, because you're going to be okay." He looked back up at the road with a fierce determination glowing in his eyes. And as he lengthened his stride, he swore to her, "We'll both be okay."

EIGHTEEN

Gentry sat in the back seat of Asher's truck cradling Blaire's head in his lap.

This was one of those moments he would never forget as long as he lived. It was like a black and white snapshot he'd seen once of his grandpa. He'd never met his grandpa because he'd died before he was born, but Gentry used to stare at the old photograph in Dad's cabin of his grandpa standing next to the inn, leaning against an old water pump with this hardened look on his face, like life had kicked the shit out of him, and that was as close to a smile as he could muster anymore. Gentry used to look at it and think it so strange that he was dead, and this was the only thing people had to remember him by.

Gentry couldn't explain it, but he got that same feeling now. Like this was the life-kicked-the-shit-out-of-me moment before he died and left no legacy. And what legacy did he even care about if Blaire wasn't around? This moment was frozen. Roman was in the passenger's seat, biting his thumb nail, staring out the window. There was no song on the radio, no talking. Asher was driving, and his profile was rigid and angry. And in the back seat, Gentry was stroking Blaire's hair out of her face. Already she was drenched in sweat. That would be the fever starting. The poison did that. He was poison.

Asher growled and tossed him a fiery look. "Cut that shit out, Gentry."

Gentry frowned, and Roman looked over at their oldest brother, too, with a confused look.

"Can you read minds now?" Gentry asked suspiciously.

"No. But I can feel your damn thoughts, and you need to keep it to yourself. You won't help her that way." Asher heaved a sigh and took a right onto a road Gentry didn't recognize. "Odine isn't what you think."

"What?" Roman asked. "How do you know about Odine?"

"Because she's the reason we have our wolves."

Gentry sat up straighter. "What do you mean?"

"Mom was human, Gentry. The three of us? We were born human. Odine gave us wolves. She tried to erase the memories, but I started having dreams about it when I was twenty. I came back looking for answers. I found Odine. I didn't realize she and Dad were a couple. I just thought she was a witch he'd hired. Now I don't think he hired her at all. I think she was a part of our lives when we were kids, and Dad asked her to make us like him so we could be part of the pack."

"Or so he could be alpha," Roman spat out. "And I'm no human. I never was, so your dreams are bullshit."

"What Odine is going to do…" Asher murmured, ignoring Roman's outburst. When he glanced at Gentry in the rearview mirror, his silver eyes looked haunted. "You won't want to be there."

"I'm not leaving my mate," Gentry growled out, his head spinning with the implications. Born human. Human? Couldn't be. Wolf was a part of him. Separate but part of him. But...that would explain why he'd chosen a human mate when he wasn't supposed to even be attracted to them. It explained why Dad had picked Odine instead of Nelda. He'd already been attracted to humans before her. He'd been attracted to his mother.

The deeper he dug into Rangeley and all the buried secrets here, the more the memories of his father flickered like old lightbulbs.

Gentry ran a light touch over the bandages on Blaire's arms. She was here because of him. Because he'd thought the Bone-Rippers were salvageable. Because he'd expected more of them. Because he'd trusted his memories more than his instinct to tuck his mate under his arm and run with her.

"I want to know," Blaire whispered. Her pupils were blown. "I want to know why you didn't kill that big gray wolf. That was Rhett, right? The man who killed your father. The man who ordered this." Her voice tapered, and her face crumpled as a tear slid out of the corner of her eye and down her cheek. "Why, Gentry?"

"Because killing Rhett would make Gentry alpha of the Bone-Rippers," Asher said. "Can't have that."

"Surely you would be a better alpha than Rhett."

Gentry shook his head. "Maybe I would've considered it if the pack hadn't gone after you like that. They hunted together though, Blaire. They hunted a human. They hunted *my* human." His voice shook with fury, and she winced. "I don't know if a single one is worth saving, but I can't put myself on the throne of monsters. We need more time."

Asher pulled up to a small cabin in the middle of nowhere. Perhaps to Blaire with her dull human senses, this place would feel like any other home, cozy even, but thick, sickening fog drifted over Gentry's skin, raising the hair all over his body. The stink of magic nearly choked him.

Roman gagged in the front seat, and when Asher looked back at Gentry, he was pale as a ghost. He waited there, as if asking Gentry if he was sure about this.

"Come on," Gentry said low. He got out and scooped Blaire into his arms. She was still awake, but just barely. She was staring at the sky, unblinking, even when snowflakes brushed her dark lashes. Her pupils were so enlarged that her eyes looked black right now. Gentry wanted to kill the entire Bone-

Ripper Pack, but revenge would have to wait.

Odine sat on the front porch, bundled in a thick wool blanket and shivering like she'd been there for a while. "Took you long enough." She admonished him behind chattering teeth. "How long since the bite?"

"How did you know?" Gentry asked, resting his boot on the bottom stair.

"She had a broken lifeline. When I traced it with my finger, in my head I had a vision flicker back and forth, back and forth. In one vision, the lifeline picked up again and continued for a long time, curved beautifully under her thumb. In the other vision, it stopped in the middle of her hand and didn't continue. It was always up to you which vision would come to fruition."

"I don't understand what that means," Gentry gritted out, good and fucking tired of riddles.

"You could come to me for the wolf, or you could watch her die. I've already been gathering supplies, but I need a few more things."

She rested her pitch-colored gaze on Asher.

"You need them alive?" he murmured, gaze averted to the snow.

"Need what alive?" Roman asked.

"I need big power to save your she-wolf," Odine said. "I need living things to draw that power from."

"Jesus," Roman muttered, pacing away, then back. "And you expect Asher to bring you these living things?"

"Yes," Odine said without hesitation. "Because I know he will."

Chills blasted up Gentry's forearms as he looked at his oldest brother. Blaire let off a pained sound, and he cradled her closer.

Odine sighed out a frustrated sound and stood on the top step. "Bring me sick animals that won't make it, or bring me something stuck in a hunter's trap." She gave Roman a dirty look. "It'll take longer, so you can help."

"No. Make Gentry help."

"Gentry is good, and I want to keep him that way," Odine snapped as she disappeared into the dark cabin. "Besides, you heard him in the car. He won't leave his mate. Now hurry, scurry, Strikers. A storm's a-comin'."

"A storm's always coming," Gentry muttered as he followed her into the cabin.

"I'm not talking about the weather."

Gentry turned in the entryway to see his brothers both standing in the snow, staring up at him with haunted looks. And then the door slammed closed.

"Fucking *rude*," Roman called through the barrier.

Gentry smiled despite how very un-funny this entire situation was. Leave it to Roman to talk to a witch like that.

"Lay her there," Odine said, gesturing to a table in the middle of a cluttered kitchen.

Above him, bundles of drying plants hung from the rafters. The counters were covered in a mismatched disarray of differently sized glass jars full of powders. The labels were printed in a language he didn't understand.

Before he did this, he had to make sure. "Blaire," he murmured, settling her on the wooden surface as Odine busied herself stoking the fire in the hearth.

"Mmm," Blaire said, staring vacantly up at the ceiling above.

"Do you want to do this? Do you want Odine to try and raise your wolf? Do you want her to try and fix this?"

Blaire rolled her head to the side and locked hollow eyes on Gentry. "Will it save you?"

Gentry swallowed hard. Of course, she would think of him instead of herself in this moment. She was walking through Hell, and her concern was saving him. She was an angel. She was everything. Already he could feel her sickness through their bond. It curdled his stomach and made Wolf crazed. If she died, he wouldn't be far behind her. If she lived…he lived. He'd always dreaded a bond, avoided women, hated the idea of his life being so tethered to another's. But now, he didn't want to live unless it was with her.

He nodded his answer.

"Then yes," she said on a breath. "I want Odine to save you."

NINETEEN

Blaire was stuck between dream and awake. She was pinned in the in-between. On one side, there were hallucinations of horrible things. Pain and monsters with sharp teeth. Something was constantly snarling right behind her. Glowing eyes in the dark. Fear.

On the other side, in lucid moments, she could see Odine working over her. She chanted things Blaire didn't understand. It smelled bad. It had to be the plants she was burning over and around her, but it smelled like something more. Death? Was that her own death she could sense? Against the wall, Gentry stood, watching over her. Always watching over her. Who was screaming? His fists were clenched.

Sometimes he looked away, but not for long. Not her Gentry. He would never leave her alone to lie here. When his lips would snarl back and he would growl, it would match the sound in her head. That's always when the clarity flickered. It was as if he was calling to the dark monster behind her, and the shadow was calling back. And it always, always sent her spiraling into the dark again.

Odine would switch to English just in time to whisper, "Let her have you," before Blaire was swallowed up by the hallucinations again.

It had been infinity, or maybe a day, or maybe a week, she didn't know. Her body was weak and needed food. There was yelling. Gentry was yelling. Someone stop that screaming! Asher was there, stone-faced, telling Gentry he needed to eat or sleep. Telling him to take a break and leave for a while. She wanted to laugh. Silly Asher. Gentry couldn't leave. They were bound, stuck together like a magnet to a paperclip. If he left, he would drag her soul with him. Gentry wouldn't leave her. He wouldn't. She wanted to bite Asher for suggesting it. Bite him? Yes, that felt right.

Roman was squatted in the corner. He looked

sick, but his face morphed from his handsome, bearded, worried face, to his snarling wolf with the gold eyes. They'd come for Gentry on that snowy road. He'd called, and they'd come. They'd come for her. Too late. The screaming was so loud in her ears, but it changed to something steady. Something with a tone that held. Something beautiful.

Blaire tried to smile. One of the boys was howling. She arched her back against the table in an effort to see which one. Which one of her boys was singing for her? Her pack was calling her home.

Gentry stood in the middle of the room, his eyes wide and reflecting strangely in the firelight. His fists weren't clenched anymore, and under his beard, he was almost...smiling. When had he grown a beard? He looked handsome in it. She wanted to touch him and kiss him and tell him everything would be okay because she was fighting for him. She was fighting to live so that he could keep breathing. So she could keep his heart beating because it was the most important sound in the world.

Near the wall, Roman had his hand on Asher's shoulder, and they both looked bewildered. Eyes too bright though, silver and gold. They weren't howling either.

Her body buckled, and the howl rose again. Her howl.

And then there was the sound of gunfire. And then there was pain.

Blaire fell off the table, or more like…she didn't fit on the table anymore. Not as she had. The clatter of bowls and the shattering of glass was deafening. She could hear everything as she scrambled against the floor, trying to ease the hurt that rippled through her body and blazed down every nerve ending.

Odine was still chanting, louder now, words that made no sense and all ran together.

"What's happening to her?" Roman asked. Too loud, too loud. His voice bounced around her skull, splitting it.

Words were impossible now, but suddenly, the pain stopped. It just disappeared like fog in the sunshine. She couldn't move. She was frozen, and her body didn't make sense. Nothing felt like it was where it was supposed to be. Something moved behind her, and she yelped a strange noise and scrambled away from it. More movement, and she went mad, clawing her way in a clumsy circle to defend herself. Roman had his cell phone up taking pictures, and Gentry was trying to calm her, hands out as he approached.

Don't! She snapped her teeth at him, and he winced away. Asher wore a dark smile as he leaned back against the wall with his arms crossed over his chest.

Odine wasn't chanting anymore. She sagged heavily into a chair as if she were utterly exhausted. She looked like she'd aged a decade, and there was more gray in her hair now. "Let her out before she finds her legs and destroys my house." Her voice cracked with age. "And for God sakes, boys, don't let her kill anyone."

"I thought werewolves didn't come in white," Roman said as Gentry threw the door to the cabin open.

Werewolf? White? Baffled, Blaire looked down at the floor, and to her horror, there were two snow-white wolf legs with black claws that had raked deep scratches into the wooden floorboards under her.

There was movement behind her again, scaring her into scrabbling forward.

"Look it," Roman crowed. "She's afraid of her

own tail."

"Shut the fuck up, man," Gentry said, shoving his brother into the wall. "She doesn't know what's happening."

"I thought she would look like a zombie or something," Asher murmured. "Red eyes maybe."

Odine snorted tiredly. "Do you look like a zombie wolf? Do you have red eyes? I made you three the same way. Now get out. I need rest."

Asher and Roman strode out the door, but Gentry knelt in front of Blaire. He looked so striking with the soft winter light filtering through the open door behind him. He didn't try to touch her with his hands, but his eyes felt like they were caressing her. So green. She could see little gold flecks in them, could see each movement of his pupil as he focused on her. He looked so relieved. No, he felt relieved. She could sense it through some invisible link that hung in the air between them.

Mine.

A slow smile stretched behind Gentry's beard. And in a reverent whisper, he said, "You're so beautiful, Trouble."

She wanted to smile, but didn't know how in this

body. Excitement built up in her body as she realized what was happening.

It had worked. Whatever Odine had done had worked.

She was alive, and because of that, Gentry—her Gentry—was alive.

He felt bigger in this body. Dominant. Intimidating even though his eyes were soft. She needed to touch him, though, so she gave into her new instincts and pushed herself forward on her belly, then rolled over on her side when she reached him, nudging her nose under his hand.

He chuckled and ran his fingertips up her muzzle. Felt so freaking good. A needy whine left her lips, and there was more movement behind her. Wagging tail, nothing to be afraid of this time.

"You want to run?" he asked through a wicked grin. He looked completely exhausted, and she should let him rest, but the excitement in her body was still there, so yes! She needed to run. That was a great suggestion. Her mate was a genius.

She tried to work her body, and shocker, she was clumsy as hell, but she got the hang of it a little by the time she reached the open door. Gentry strode behind her, pulling off his shirt. Sexy mate. Blaire fell all the way down the stairs with a yelp. Gentry laughed.

On the edge of the woods were two wolves—one black as tar with white eyes, and one gray and brown with eyes the color of melted gold. Pack. Strikers. She was one of them now. They thought they were going to leave Gentry, leave her, but she wouldn't let them. She was going to make them jump the right side of the fence.

Bouncing unsteadily, she aimed for them. Roman huffed a sneeze that sounded suspiciously like a wolf laugh. Jerk. Asher blinked slowly and made her walk all the way to him, lowering herself like she'd done with Gentry because the Strikers felt scary. She was basically camouflaged into the snow with just her ears poking out when Asher finally sniffed her once and then trotted away, apparently bored. Jerk number two. She liked them.

A blur of gray blasted past her, then Gentry skidded to a stop and circled back, running so fast it shocked her to stillness. And right when she thought he would plow into her, he leapt into the air and sailed right over her with a grace that stole her breath away. Behind her, he was down on his front end, his butt up in the air, his tail wagging slowly, his tongue out.

Play with me.

She liked playing! Blaire took off, concentrating on her feet until she got the hang of running. And then Gentry was right there running beside her, racing her. On either side of them, Asher and Roman ran through the woods, eyes drifting to Blaire time and time again.

Mine, all mine, my Gentry, my life, my boys, my Strikers, my pack, my snow, my woods, my wolf. She wanted to scream and laugh and cry and then start all over again. Blaire felt insane with how powerful and fast this body was. The pads of her feet barely made any sound as she sprinted through the snow, around trees and brush, weaving in and out with the other wolves now.

Everything was going to be okay.

Emotion overwhelmed her. She locked her long legs and skidded to a stop in a clearing. Gentry reached her first, worry pooling in his glowing green eyes. He clamped his teeth on her neck when she ducked to the ground for him, but it didn't hurt. Love bite. He sniffed her fur as she lay there, then flopped over on top of her, rubbing his back on her like he had an itch. Felt good. He was so warm. Happiness trilled through the bond, and now the emotion that had stopped her swelled. She wanted to cry but didn't have the luxury of that outlet in this body. She couldn't absorb this all-consuming feeling in her body, so she closed her eyes and sang. It was a short howl, unpracticed. But Gentry stood in a rush right above her, tossed his head back, and cried out, too. His voice was deeper and started low, then rose by an octave and held. Stunning.

When Roman howled, he sounded different from Gentry. She committed his tone to memory and sang again with him and Gentry. Asher waited so long she thought he wouldn't join in, but as the tightness in her chest finally eased, he lifted his head and cried out to the winds and the woods and the sky.

This was a declaration. And not just Asher's. Blaire could almost hear their thoughts, hear the meaning behind this song. A mash-up of jumbled words rattled around in her head, and for the life of her, she couldn't figure out if she was making them up or if the three wolves standing so near were talking. *I'm staying. We have to stay. I'm staying, too. Just for a while. Not ready to go. Things left unfinished. Not this time.*

She was glad Gentry hadn't killed Rhett now. This moment wouldn't have existed if he had. He would've been alpha of that awful pack, and Asher and Roman would be scattered to the wind. And she, by default, would've been a Bone-Ripper, just like the bloodthirsty animals that had tried and failed to kill her.

Her clever mate had known what he was doing.

Gentry had separated the Strikers from the monsters and separated her from the darkness. They'd saved each other, but he'd gone above and beyond what she could've ever imagined. He'd brought her from the brink time and time again when she was fighting for her life in Odine's cabin. He'd called to her wolf when she got weak, called to her protective instincts, called for her to come back to him.

She was no longer weak, frail, and weaponless in a place where supernaturals ruled the shadows.

Gentry had gone to war with an entire pack for her life.

And then his love had made her into the white wolf of Winter's Edge.

EPILOGUE

Well, no one would ever be able to call Blaire boring again. Her eyes were glowing like green bug lights, and the snarl in her chest was constant. Matt would crap a brick if he saw her like this.

While she slathered on another layer of lip-gloss in the pull-down mirror of Gentry's new truck, stalling like a champ, Roman laughed like a psychopath behind her. From the familiar audio on the phone, she wanted to strangle him.

"Look at this," he said, shoving his phone toward her. "Look how dumb you look trying to run from your own tail." Butthole had taken video in Odine's cabin.

With an eyeroll, Blaire shoved his hand away.

She secretly adored Asher and Roman, but she also secretly wanted to strangle them several times a day.

"It'll be fine," Gentry said, sliding his hand over her thigh. "There won't be any humans in there tonight, so if you lose it a little, it's no big deal."

She'd prepped for this by Changing earlier and letting her wolf run wild for a few hours, but she still wasn't confident in her ability to control the animal side of her. It had been two weeks since Odine had raised her wolf and saved her life. Two weeks tucked away and hidden in Hunter Cove until she had more control. Two weeks of begging her boss to let her work from home and explaining to Ashlyn she hadn't been kidnapped, but that she found a place she wanted to stay. Blaire grinned. Two incredible weeks of getting to spend time with Gentry fixing the inn and cleaning up Winter's Edge. Two weeks of nights curled up against him in his bed. Her old life felt so far away now. It felt as if she'd ditched all the parts of herself she'd grown disappointed in and clung to the pieces she liked. She was the best version of herself here in Rangeley. Stronger, more confident, more capable of enjoying the moment and not focusing on losing herself in work just to make it to the next day.

Here, with Gentry, she was ardently happy.

But she couldn't remain hidden in the Hunter Cove Inn for the rest of her life, so tonight was the first night of her new life.

Blaire narrowed her eyes on the Four Horsemen with determination and sighed to expel the rest of her nerves. "I'm ready."

"About time," Roman said, shoving his phone into his pocket. "I've been trying to annoy you out of the truck for half an hour. I need a drink."

Asher was already out of the truck and making his way to the tavern, his hands shoved into his pockets. Roman slammed the door and jogged after him. He clapped Asher on the back, which got him a hard shove in the shoulder from the quietest of the Striker brothers. So, everything wasn't perfect. The brothers still fought like cats and dogs, and not a day went by where they didn't end up in a fist fight or a wolf-fight, but at least they wouldn't kill each other now. Probably.

Gentry helped her out of the truck, but he didn't lead her inside right away. Instead, he pulled her against his chest and buried his face against her neck. "Are you happy?"

"Silly wolf, of course I'm happy. Can't you feel it?"

"Not tonight."

Oh. Blaire slid her arms around his neck and held him tight, scratched the back of his neck gently as she stared up at the starry sky. "I'm nervous right now, but I'll be okay again when I don't feel like there is this huge weight hanging over us. Odine said my lifeline is long and strong now. And yeah, I didn't believe in that stuff before, but everything is different now. I'm here, with you, where I'm supposed to be. Now we just need to go secure my place in this town."

Gentry eased back and gripped her waist, leveling her with a look. There was promise in his voice when he murmured, "I won't let anything happen to you, Trouble."

And she believed him. How could she not? She'd watched him fight the Bone-Rippers for her life at the risk of his own. He would have her back always, just like she would have his. His devotion rang clear as a bell through their bond, and she fell in love with him even more.

Gentry leaned into her, pushing her back slowly until her shoulder blades hit the side of his truck. And with a wicked smile she found so sexy, he kissed her.

This one was a soft one, where their lips moved slowly against each other. He angled his face the other way and brushed his tongue against the closed seam of her lips as he cupped her neck and touched her cheek with his thumb. Gentle Gentry, a beast in war, a fighter, a protector, but with her, he was tender. Hard where he needed to be for his family and for this town, but easy with her.

She didn't know how she'd gotten this lucky, but she would work to make him feel her devotion back. Odine had once said she was meant to guide him to his potential, and that witch was right most of the time. But Blaire couldn't help but feel like it was Gentry who was leading Blaire to hers.

Gentry pushed his tongue against hers in gentle strokes that made her melt into his warmth. She would never get tired of this feeling of safety he always enveloped her with.

A sharp whistle sounded from the Four Horsemen, and Gentry growled against her mouth before he rolled his head toward Roman, who was standing impatiently in the open doorway of the tavern.

Roman arched both eyebrows up and glared at

them. "That's just great that you're both making out while I'm in here trying to keep Asher from murdering everyone."

"Right. Business first, making out later," she teased. Asher probably would murder the Bone-Rippers if they pushed him enough.

Gentry grabbed her hand and jogged toward the open door, his breath freezing in front of his face. When he cast her a bright-eyed glance over his shoulder, she was struck with how handsome her mate was when he smiled like this—the easy kind that he only did for her.

"You ready to stir up some trouble, Trouble?" he asked.

"Ready," she said breathlessly as she followed him inside.

Gentry's wide shoulders were blocking her from the loud room, but the second he stepped to the side and she laid eyes on the werewolves gathered there, the noise dropped to dead silence and everyone froze.

"Holy, fuck," a man in his thirties said from where he held a dart up in mid-air, ready to release it at a board on the wall. "You're supposed to be dead."

Blaire smiled brightly. "You assholes turned me into one of you instead. Congrats. You failed epically. I need a drink."

"Whisky?" Roman asked hopefully from behind the bar, where he had apparently decided to play bartender.

"Ew. No. Something sweet."

"Does not compute," Roman said, dramatically pouring whisky into a row of shot glasses.

Blaire balked at everyone staring at her, but Gentry guided her toward the bar with his fingertips pressed against her lower back. She sat on a bar stool between Asher and a man who had visited her nightmares. She'd seen his unlaced boots that night the truck had flipped. The night she'd been hunted by wolves. The night her human self had died. Rhett.

She dared to meet his eyes so he could see how very un-human she was now. So he could see his failure to snuff her out.

Gentry locked his arms on the bar top on either side of her and kissed her neck, sucking gently. She stifled the growl in her throat and leaned back into her mate. If he wasn't worried, she wouldn't be either. With her whole heart, she trusted Gentry.

He moved his kisses upward, bit her earlobe gently, and then angled his face toward Rhett. "You look like shit."

Indeed, he did. Rhett hadn't healed very well from where Gentry had worked his throat over, and he was hunched and pale as he nursed a half-full beer.

"What are you doing in my bar, Strikers?" he asked in a hoarse voice. He looked tired and slow, but he still felt heavy enough that Blaire stayed wary.

"Your bar?" Roman asked, passing out shots. "Didn't know your name was on the lease, but okay. We'll pick a different bar next time."

"This is the only bar in town," a dark-haired woman said quietly from where she stood, hands clasped in front of her, chin to her chest, eyes wary and on Roman.

"False, Mila. You look hot by the way. Grew up right, nice tits. Bad choice in friends though," Roman said, the humor melting from his voice. "We're here with announcements. Four announcements to be precise."

"What announcements?" Rhett ground out. Oh, his eyes were glowing now, and he felt so much heavier.

"One," Gentry said, gaze locked on the alpha's. "Blaire's alive. If at any point anyone here feels like that should change, I will burn your mother-fucking pack to the ground."

"I will also do the mother-fucking burning," Roman said, lifting two fingers.

"Same," Asher said as he stared at Rhett with dead eyes.

"Also same," Blaire chirped up. "I have teeth and murdery instincts now."

"That's my girl," Gentry murmured and kissed her temple. "Two. Winter's Edge will be re-opening within the week. It was the bar this pack hung out at back when you were great. All are welcome. Three."

"Oh, I like three," Roman said, his eyes flashing with excitement.

"Me, too," Blaire agreed.

"Three..." The smile dipped from Gentry's face, and he glared at Rhett. "This isn't over. I don't want your pack, but you killed our dad, and then you tried to kill my mate. Don't take my lenience the other day for weakness, *alpha*. I'm just more patient at hunting than you are."

"A toast to Rhett croaking," Roman said, lifting his shot glass.

Blaire giggled and lifted hers along with Gentry and Asher. "Croak!" She tapped the bottom of the glass on the bar top, then tossed it back. It was disgusting and made her eyes water, but she was tough about it.

Gentry hooked an arm around her waist and kissed her quick but deep. Just enough tongue to make her dizzy with lust, and then he was leading her back out of the bar behind Roman and Asher. The Strikers were giants among men, confident in their strides as they walked out unhurried.

The buzz behind them grew until Rhett called out in a snarl, "What's the last one? You said there were four announcements."

Gentry turned at the door and gave a feral smile. "Four. There's a new pack in town."

"You're reviving the Striker Pack?" Mila asked timidly from the back of the bar.

"No," Gentry answered, pulling Blaire against him, side-by-side, just as they'd stood in the street surrounded by the Bone-Rippers. Side-by-side facing the fray together, now and always. Odine said there was a storm a-comin', and she was right. "The Striker Pack died with my father," Gentry said. "We're the Wolves of Winter's Edge."

Want more of these characters?

Gentry is the first book in a three book standalone series called Wolves of Winter's Edge.

For more of these characters, check out these other books from T. S. Joyce.

Roman
(Wolves of Winter's Edge, Book 2)

Asher
(Wolves of Winter's Edge, Book 3)

About the Author

T.S. Joyce is devoted to bringing hot shifter romances to readers. Hungry alpha males are her calling card, and the wilder the men, the more she'll make them pour their hearts out. She werebear swears there'll be no swooning heroines in her books. It takes tough-as-nails women to handle her shifters.

Experienced at handling an alpha male of her own, she lives in a tiny town, outside of a tiny city, and devotes her life to writing big stories. Foodie, wolf whisperer, ninja, thief of tiny bottles of awesome smelling hotel shampoo, nap connoisseur, movie fanatic, and zombie slayer, and most of this bio is true.

Bear Shifters? Check

Smoldering Alpha Hotness? Double Check

Sexy Scenes? Fasten up your girdles, ladies and gents, it's gonna to be a wild ride.

For more information on T. S. Joyce's work,
visit her website at
www.tsjoyce.com

Made in the USA
Middletown, DE
18 December 2016